Seeking Signs

Staci Angelina Mercado

Four
Feathers
Press

Seeking Signs
By Staci Angelina Mercado
Author blog: staciangelinamercado.com

For permission requests, contact the publisher:

 Four Feathers Press
fourfeatherspress@gmail.com
Printed in the U.S.A.

First Edition
Library of Congress Cataloging-in-Publication Data
Mercado, Staci
Seeking Signs

ISBN-13 978-0615830810
ISBN-10 0615830811

1. Historical Fiction—Iowa—1900-1913 2. Juvenile Fiction
3. Mystery—Fiction 4. Iowa—Fiction 5. Death—Fiction 6. Storytelling—Fiction 7. German-Americans—Fiction

10 9 8 7 6 5 4 3 2 1

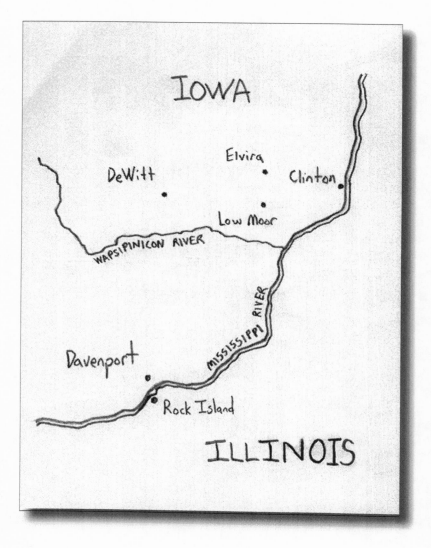

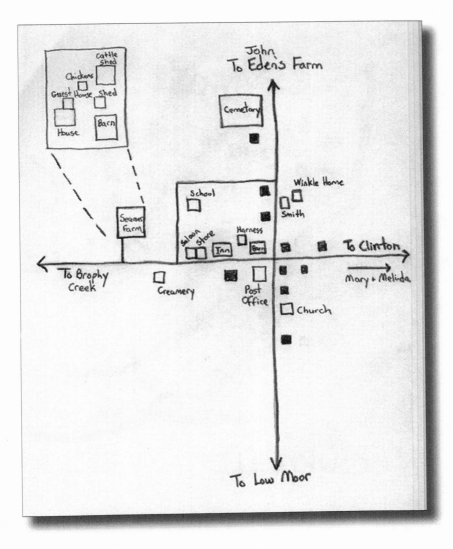

For all those curious enough to seek.

Prologue

In sure and certain hope of the resurrection to eternal life through our Lord Jesus Christ, we commend to Almighty God our sister Wilhelmina Mary Seamer, and we commit her body to the ground; earth to earth; ashes to ashes, dust to dust. The Lord bless her and keep her; the Lord make his face to shine upon her and be gracious unto her and give her peace. Amen.

A slow trickle of sweat began at the base of my neck and slid down to the small of my back. It was hot, hot, hot. To add to it, I felt dull cramps in my stomach all morning. I wasn't sure of the cause... nerves, perhaps... and grief. The kind of grief that settles on you like a damp, heavy blanket. No matter how hard you try to work yourself out from that blanket, it only adds weight, and form, and more grief. During the burial, the full, ugly brunt of my sister's death washed over me and erased my childhood. I knew it fully. *My sister did not kill herself.* Up until that point, the thought was just something I played at. A fantasy. Like denial that someone is dead, except this denial was in the manner of the death. It was something to hold on to; I couldn't imagine that someone could kill herself. Especially not my sister, my second mother, my friend. Someone killed *her*. Someone *killed* her. Just then, the grass turned black, the priest turned white. A flock of grey sparrows passed from tree to tree in a frenzy. The sky... the ... My brother John held out to me a handkerchief blazing white in the sun... and I fell, awkwardly and suddenly, into his arms.

* * * * *

I became a private investigator the day my sister died. Never mind that I was only a girl of 13 and she was 32. *Thirteen* and *a girl* is just as good as anything else. All you need is common sense, the ability to observe things, and some sneak in you. To tell you the truth, my age and the fact that I was a girl helped me blend in and appear harmless to the one who killed her. At least for a while, anyway. Things did go badly in the end.

A private investigator by the name of Phinny stayed in our family's hotel a couple of weeks before my sister died. He was tracking counterfeiters. They were all over the United States on account of all the national banks printing their own money and all. I guess it was easy to fake bills during those days, and he was hired by Clinton National Bank to handle a big case.

My job at our hotel was to serve drinks to the customers and clear tables. While I worked, Phinny told me all about Maxwell Shrift — the infamous counterfeiter who made his way across the Midwest. He told me about nearly nabbing him on the electric car between here and Lyons township. "Had my hand right on his shirt collar," he claimed. "Now it'll be months before I find him again." I showed so much interest in his profession that Phinny gave me a booklet from the investigative school he attended several years before. "This will get you started," he said with a wink. "Take notes on everything." Little did he know that little something would help me solve a murder.

The booklet is titled "The Baum Detective Agency Course." Okay, so I realize I didn't actually attend the class itself; the summaries helped steer me in the right direction is all. It's also kind of like the table of contents for this book if you want to know the truth. The rest is just the common sense that I was telling you about.

From the World's Greatest Investigative School

The Baum Detective Agency Course

Observation - Know what and when to observe. How can you use your eyes and ears?

Memory - Look back at all the important moments. What can you recall that may be meaningful?

Description - Familiarize yourself with the known facts and be able to write them down. What is fact and what is opinion?

Gaining Confidences - All great investigators know where to look for help. One cannot do this alone. Who might be able to get you the information you need?

Trust Your Instincts - Most of the time, your instincts are correct. What is your gut telling you?

Gathering Evidence - Hunt for evidence in wastebaskets, drawers, closets, books, and pockets. Where else can you look?

Investigating - Sometimes a detective may have to accept certain uncomfortable realities. Are you ready to discover the truth?

Shadowing - You may need to follow suspects for a time to gain information. How can you do this without being detected?

Inspecting Places - If there is a crime involved, the scene of the crime must be explored. What can you find there?

Self - defense - Expect to get into dangerous situations. What should you do when you have to protect yourself?

The Bigger Picture - Yours is one perspective. Keep looking for more. What is the whole story?

Observation

Know what and when to observe. How can you use your eyes and ears?

"He won't be the best in the game any more," the old German woman mumbled. Deep grooves criss-crossed her face and offered evidence of her years.

My older sister Minnie and I stole a quick glance at one another while watching the woman paint a picture outside of her tent at the Clinton County Fair. In it, twelve crows flew across a sunset sky and a thirteenth dove for the ground. When she finished the last bird, the woman looked straight at us and shook her paintbrush. A small speck of black paint flew and landed at Minnie's feet.

"You must learn to watch for the signs. There are always signs. If you can read the signs, you can change the way."

With that, the woman gathered her long black skirt and hobbled back into her tent. Long, gray hair sprang out from her haphazard bun and the sharp smell of her paints wafted into my nose as the tent flap sealed her off from my curiosity.

"What was that about?" I asked.

"I don't know… but let's not think about it! We should get to the grandstands soon; they'll be filling up. He should be here in a few hours, and you know how everyone gets everywhere early! We'll want a seat in the shade."

"The Lord knows it's awful hot and sticky today!" I whined, pulling the back of my dress away from my sweaty skin.

Minnie grabbed my arm, and we slowly made our way through the thoroughfare and throngs of people in their Sunday best. The biggest attraction of the day was the pilot Louis Rosenbaum who planned a flight all the way from Indiana to our county fair. He'd been all over the country and even gave a demonstration to President Taft. We were lucky, to be sure. No one I knew had ever seen an aeroplane before. It was a modern miracle. My excitement was so great the stomach butterflies reached all the way up to my heart. We weaved in and out of people we knew, absentmindedly nodding here and there with a how-do-you-do for politeness.

There were at least 500 people in the main thoroughfare alone, and travel through them was not easy. We gently elbowed our way through and sidled between groups of folks catching up on events and fathers playing penny games to win trinkets for eager sons and daughters. A swarm of dirty boys barreled their way through the crowd and knocked me to the ground, adding dirt to my sweaty dress. The smallest one backpedaled his way through the crowd and gave me a sneer. I called to Minnie to pause a minute. She looked back and seeing me with my rear on the ground, stretched out her hand.

"Boys!" Minnie laughed, and pulled me to my feet. "Don't worry about the dirt. No one will notice." She brushed off the back of my dress with quick hands. When I looked up, the stilt walking man emerged from between two tents and began to pick his way through the crowd ahead of us. Nervous mothers grabbed the hands of little ones and scuttled away while country gentlemen tipped their hats and moved aside for him. "Look! The crowd's getting out of the way," I pointed out.

"Let's go!" Minnie picked up on my meaning right away as an easy path emerged before us and we floated along in the stilt walker's wake.

Outside a large tent, young men clamored for their turn posing in the new Mercer Raceabout — top speed 80 mph! A middle-aged photographer and his female assistant attempted to control the crowd with efficiency and humor as they produced picture postcards to undoubtedly impress the girls, some of whom giggled in the entryway.

The newest Indian motorcycles brought in groups of men and

women alike underneath the cool shade of the next tent. Admiring eyes raked their way over the contours of the latest and fastest motorcycle around.

A boxing demonstration held by the Boys Club of DeWitt got a bit out of hand when what was supposed to be a light jab turned out to be a strong punch to a now-bloody nose. The battered boy swung his way back with a vengeance as the sponsors attempted to pull them apart. Snickers rippled through the crowd and families got up to leave.

"What about William? Won't he want to sit with us?" I asked, my attention back on our destination.

"Sakes! I forgot all about him. We'll stop in at the beer tent. He's sure to be inside or somewhere thereabouts."

William, Minnie's husband, stood talking to a group of six men, all of whom held mugs of malt beer and were laughing at something William said. I recognized one of the men — he was the sheriff of Clinton County. His badge twinkled in the sunlight.

"Run on over and see if William wants to come with us," Minnie instructed me. She was acting the lady, and ladies didn't go into beer tents. I tried to wait patiently as William finished his story, but I didn't think he saw me, so I poked him in the arm. He finished his sentence off with a laugh and I felt the eyes of each of the men on me. Dropping my face to the ground I said, "Minnie wants to know if you want to sit with us in the grandstands. The flying machine will be here soon."

"You gals go on ahead," William assured me. "I'll be along shortly and look for you. If there's no room, I'll just stand down below."

I skipped back to Minnie and informed her of William's plans. We half ran, half walked the rest of the way to the grandstands. We weren't the only ones eager to get an early seat. Families, old couples, young people on dates, and the hoard of boys who knocked me down all clambered up the sturdy wooden benches and jockeyed for position in the upper rows — safe from the summer sun under the newly constructed roof. Minnie and I chose our spot near the top and I don't know who was squirmier. Minnie was quite a bit older than I was; she was like a second mother to me, but yet, she felt like one of my best school friends that day.

We spent the time talking about what it must be like to fly. Imagine soaring alongside birds or above them even! We talked about where we would go if we could travel anywhere. I longed to see lines of elephants trudging through the dust on their way to a watering hole, tall, lanky giraffes nibbling on the leaves in the topmost branches of trees, and lazy lions in the shade, yawning with content bellies, blood still on their lips. A slight breeze picked up and ruffled my hair and dress. I imagined the breeze was that of the African savannah as I, the first female pilot in the history of everywhere, flew across an entire continent. I trailed off in my thoughts, imagining all sorts of near-peril to add drama to my adventures.

"The Taj Mahal!" Minnie crooned as she brought me back to a different world. "That's where I'd like to go! Have you heard the story of it?"

"No! Tell me!"

"Well, it's a romantic one to be sure — but sad. A magnificent mausoleum was built by emperor Shah Jahan in honor of his wife, Mumtaz Mahal, who died giving birth to their fourteenth child. Imagine! She was so strong as to give him fourteen children! His love for her was so great that he thought to honor her with the most beautiful man-made structure ever built. Near the banks of the river Yamuna rises the Taj Mahal. To get there you must pass through the great gate, which is really another building itself, more magnificent than any we've ever seen. Once you walk through, a long, tree-lined reflecting pool and lush gardens mark the path. And there, on a giant pedestal, the Taj Mahal reaches more than 110 feet into the sky. Its uppermost feature is the dome at the top — it swells with love for her. Smaller domes, balconies, minarets, and carvings adorn the outside. One could get lost in the vast rooms and hallways. And somewhere in there, lie the bodies of Shah Jahan and his wife. Their spirits roam the halls walking hand in hand for all eternity. It is said that should a sinner make his way to this mansion, all his past sins are to be washed away. I would fly *there*. And maybe the spirit of Mumtaz Mahal would bless me with fourteen children!"

I knew that Minnie was desperate for a baby. No one needed to tell me that, although I'd heard Mama and my other sisters talking about it plenty. Minnie would make a wonderful mother someday. I hoped.

When we broke away from our dreaming, I noticed how the crowd filled in. People in the lower rows motioned for stragglers to wedge into the few remaining spots in the grandstands; couples and families sat on blankets in the grass on each side. A button-box polka band walked out to a wooden platform at the base of the stands and raised the spirits of the crowd with "Spaghetti Polka." As Mr. Rosenbaum was to fly all the way from Indiana, no one knew for sure when he was to arrive. The polka band played on and on, and Minnie and I remained silent with anticipation.

Then someone shouted and ripples of attentive faces turned to the east. Cut off in mid-note, the polka band quickly scuttled away and off to the side. Murmurs arose here and there throughout the crowd and the distant buzz of the aeroplane grew louder and louder in perfect sync with my excitement. It truly was a miracle. The machine looked light as a sparrow's feather although I knew it must have been heavier than the air it floated upon. Slight tips to one side and the other made it appear fragile and precarious, but thoughts of disaster were not on my mind as the aeroplane tilted a mite haphazardly down to the dirt path constructed for it. The crowd cheered as the flying machine landed and made its way around the loop.

After he brought the aeroplane to a stop, Mr. Rosenbaum fiddled with the controls and hopped his way out to a standing ovation from the crowd. He took off his goggles and what looked like a football cap and advanced to shake hands with the mayor and a few other notables who were there to greet him formally. The men walked over the wooden platform and paused for the crowd to settle.

The mayor of DeWitt began, "Ladies, gentlemen, and children... may I present to you, Mr. Louis Rosenbaum!"

The crowd cheered and clapped, smiles all around. My heart pounded in my chest, and Minnie and I looked at one another — thoughts of the Taj Mahal alive in her eyes and Africa in mine.

Then Mr. Rosenbaum stepped forward with a shy smile, his hat and goggles still in his left hand. Was he handsome! Maybe 25, he looked like a businessman out for a leisurely Sunday walk, with his white shirt-sleeves rolled up to his elbows and black pants and vest. The wind picked up again and blew his light-brown hair as he politely waited for the crowd to quiet down.

"Hello, Clinton County!" he began.

The crowd clapped in answer to him.

Raising his free hand he chuckled a bit and waited again for quiet. "Welcome to the modern age! The time for new inventions is ripe, and although this may be the first time many of you have seen such a craft, it certainly won't be the last. Every day, pioneers around the world are improving the speed, agility, and accuracy of flight. Men like Otto Lilienthal of Germany" — and here, the crowd smiled and nodded in recognition, for most of our families were from the Old Country — "continued the work of the earliest inventors and brought us a glider that could fly a man for long distances. Inspired by this great man, Orville and Wilbur Wright developed a propulsion system with the ability to fly a craft heavier than air. And today, men everywhere continue to test the limits of knowledge and fantasy. Someday, I predict each of your sons and daughters will ride in one of these amazing machines as they travel across borders into the places of their dreams!"

Mr. Rosenbaum raised his hands in the air, his goggles bouncing, and incited the crowd to more applause as we rose to our feet once again. Then, he turned to the mayor and the other men on stage with him, and he was led back down to the aeroplane where they paused for a picture. Mr. Rosenbaum rested his elbows back on the frame of the craft and squinted against the western sun. When the photograph was taken, the men exchanged a few words, unheard by the crowd, and then the airman jogged up close to us holding up his hand once again, for quiet.

"I'll give you a demonstration of take-off and turning ability. Then I will be happy to pose for more pictures!" With that, he returned quickly to his craft, and upon starting up the engine, donned the cap and goggles, waved at the excited crowd, and pulled his way out around to the strip he landed on before.

The engine sputtered a bit, and Minnie and I glanced at one another. She grabbed for my hand in anticipation. The engine gathered its resolve, and Rosenbaum assured the crowd with another wave as he picked up speed. A few hundred yards later, he was in the air. Minnie and I realized that our position was no longer ideal, for we couldn't see the aeroplane at all from our spot high in the covered stands. Our necks craned for a view but to no avail. Dozens of people in the stands began to descend.

"Let's go!" Minnie decided. "I can tolerate a little sun for this!"

And so we made our way down to the double-sided stairs where we spotted William standing with the sheriff on the grassy slope.

"Wanted a better view, I see?" William smirked as we approached. "Isn't it something?"

Minnie began to reply but just then noticed the craft off in the distance as it made a wide turn on its way back to us. "Oh, there he is!" she cried.

"Where? I can't see!"

"Come on!" William encouraged with a flick of his wrist, and motioned for me to move closer. He pointed me in the right direction... and then I saw.

Mr. Rosenbaum flew like an eagle making one more wide turn before his descent. The sun glimmered behind him, crickets singing in the lowering light. The landing was the best part, for it was the most dangerous, and it was then that I could see his handsome face, determined and courageous. He landed only to take off again immediately; the crowd roared with appreciation.

His aeroplane launched a quick ascent, and a moment later the engine sputtered an argument. We all hushed immediately and heard the engine protest twice more before it gave up entirely. I believe that time slowed down just then. Stretched. We watched in horror as the left wing of the plane ducked down underneath the cockpit. It continued its rotation until Rosenbaum was completely upside down, and then the machine began a quick, uncontrolled plunge to the ground.

A woman in the crowd screamed.

Other cries and unintelligible murmurs roared through the onlookers until the last seconds when we were all too shocked to speak. Amidst the chaos and fear, angry crows flew across our vision and landed in the grass beyond. Thirteen of them cawed and jabbed at one another while battling for scraps of food the fair-goers left behind. The sweat dripped down my back and stopped where William's arm held me to him.

Minnie covered her eyes, and I involuntarily turned my face toward William's shoulder as Louis Rosenbaum fell to his death. The beautiful craft came down in a torrent of twisted wood and metal. Its fragile frame was reduced to a pile of rubble. I covered my ears, but my hands could not block out the horrid crunching sound. Somewhere in that pile was the man who spoke to us only moments before. I didn't want to face it. Death was not new to me, but witnessing the moment of it was, and I began to tremble as if it were winter and not a hot, Iowa summer.

William placed me down quickly as he, the sheriff, and a dozen other men ran to the wreckage. Women held their gloved hands to their mouths, and some children began to sob. We watched the men run up to the splintered craft and quickly turn their heads away with the dreaded assurance that the man was dead. William crouched and placed his jacket over Rosenbaum's head.

"Oh, no… oh, no," Minnie moaned, shaking her head in disbelief. Her eyes began to tear up, and I looked quickly away from her, for sorrow was private. A sign hung on a nearby post drew in my attention. It announced Rosenbaum's appearance today complete with a photo of the man himself in front of the same aeroplane that killed him. I walked over to the sign thinking that I would keep it to remember him by when I read, "Come see Louis Rosenbaum! The best pilot in the game!"

That's when Minnie came up behind me and I heard her repeat the words the ancient German woman said only hours before, "He won't be the best in the game anymore."

May 1905

"Much ado about nothing."
                    —William Shakespeare

Do you ever feel as if you
Might be crazy?

Just a little bit,
Or sometimes —
Given the light,
And the time of
Day?

But all of that is
Over now
In the past
Find your way out of it
Papa says

And so William
Asks me to marry him
And I wonder
Is this the way back
To the light?

July 1905

I must admit; I am hopelessly homesick. I can't fake cheerfulness today. I'm just blue. William has done his best to make sure that I am comfortable. He has allowed me a generous sum with which to purchase furnishings for the house. I had so much fun looking in the Sears and Roebuck catalog. Now that the things have arrived, I realize that they are just, after all, things. Textured wallpaper and a drop-leaf desk cannot replace the familiar shouts of the peanut sellers in town, the joyous bands that play every Friday night, and most of all — my family! I miss them all desperately!

Our lively family suppers at the Inn have been replaced by the quiet scrape of fork and knife. I try to start conversations with William, but he's not fond of it at mealtime, or any time for that matter. I don't think he even tastes his food; he eats it so fast! I find I've barely sat down and he's pushing his chair back from the table, taking out his pipe, and heading outside. I know William's not much of a talking man. I appreciate that about him. Some just don't know when to stop hearing themselves, but when I'm lonely, I long for talk.

Things are so very different here. I must think ahead. I cannot just run down to Theo's store if the need arises. I need to predict it two weeks in advance. I don't get in to Clinton any more than that. The general store in Elvira has next to nothing. If I run out of things, I'm not nearly as good as Mama at improvising!

Oh! My mouth just started to water at the thought of Mama's Monday morning bread. Nothing got me out of bed quicker than the inviting smell of it. Try as I might, I cannot get the hang of making it, either. I don't know how she makes 11 loaves without once stopping to measure anything. I can't even make one to taste as good as hers. I'm sure that she must insert a special magic into it to get it to taste so good!

I feel spoiled and rotten to go on so. I have a good life here. I just need to get used to the change.

August 1905

William is trying to turn me into a country girl. He thinks it quite necessary that I learn to take care of some of the animals. I suppose he is right. If he is away it will come upon me to do it. We have started with feeding the geese. There isn't enough grass in the yard to keep them well, so I need to fill their bucket with wheat every day. Very simple, but I wouldn't have known it needed to be done. The geese have free range of the yard and appear to get along quite well on their own.

The big male doesn't seem to like me much. He thinks he is king of the yard and lets me know about it. He'll come charging after me if I am late getting him fed. This morning there was a rat in their wheat bucket. He didn't like that, of course, so pulled a pair of my bloomers right off the clothes line and ran around with them until they were dragged entirely through with mud. William thought it was quite funny to see me chasing a goose all over the yard after my bloomers. I suppose it was funny! Even so, I'm imagining a fine goose for Christmas dinner this year.

As the sun set on our farm this evening, I sat on the porch steps and watched a dozen lazy bees hover among the flowers. William came out and sat with me. We had a short talk about our plans for the future. He wants children badly, and you know I do.

I should like my family to come for a visit one of these Sundays. I wonder if Mama and Papa would come for a picnic? I would make my fried chicken and we'd have plenty of fresh vegetables from the garden. If Mama would bring a few loaves of bread, it would cheer me up indefinitely!

I'm not sure if it was tradition or curiosity that brought us back, but there we were in William's car, traveling down the dusty country road on the way to DeWitt for the last day of the county fair.

"That poor man. I keep thinking about it," Minnie said.

"I've never seen anyone die before."

"Won't be the last time," William mumbled.

"William!" Minnie began, but stopped.

Well, I suppose I knew that and wanted to say so, but remembered Mama's backhand in response to sass and kept my mouth shut. Not that she was there in the car with us, but Mama's lessons had a way of sticking in my craw even when she wasn't around.

"William has seen more than his fair share." Minnie patted his arm. I remembered Mama said that all of William's family was gone. Sickness and disease took them all, that and hard work and long winters. William was the only one left. As a young man he learned quickly how to make his way in the world and look out for himself. "That man knows business," Papa said about William more than once.

We fell into a long silence then. William's Model T chugged along the lonely dirt road and kicked up ghostly plumes of dust that rolled off to the east behind us. It tickled the foxtail swaying in the breeze and weighed heavily on the nodding purple cone-flower, dragging the petals down with the weight of it. The dust coated the plant life so thoroughly that the colors were muted and mere shadows of their former beauty.

Red-winged blackbirds flitted up from the deep ditch grasses to keep an eye on us and landed hastily upon fenceposts calling, "See–yeeeee, see–yeeeee!" A warning for the others that a predator was near. That sound always reminded me of Minnie. The only time I heard them was in the country; they don't much like the hustle and bustle of the cities and towns, but prefer the man-made ditches disturbed only occasionally by a passing car or prowling tomcat.

Sometimes, when I'd stay with Minnie we'd go out for a walk in the country after supper — just Minnie and I and the blackbirds. Now I appreciate their diligence in protecting the fledglings hidden among thistle and milkweed, but my first encounter with a red-winged blackbird scared the living daylights out of me.

"Want to see how many seconds it takes me to reach the crossroads?" I asked as we made the turn back to Elvira.

"I'll count. You go on three!"

I stopped in my tracks and poised myself for a fast start, crouched down with my hands on one knee. I took a big breath and burst from my position when Minnie called, "Three!" My back leg slipped slightly in the smooth track worn down in the road. I righted myself and sprinted for all I was worth, determined to get there in a time worthy of praise.

I was a good ten seconds into the sprint when I heard Minnie shouting to me, but I paid her no mind, assuming she was only cheering me on. I felt an awkward breeze at my ear, frantic and warning in its proximity. I saw him out of the corner of my eye, but wasn't sure what I was seeing until I felt the flutter of wings in my hair and felt him peck the side of my head two or three times before my wildly flailing arms were able to scatter the resolve of a lone male red-wing attempting to protect his young. Hidden among the ditch weeds were two or three small, grey, desperate chicks, hungry for a meal. Somewhere nearby, its camouflaged brown mate perched with her eyes on me but safe by a fencepost and panting. Minnie came running up next to me, laughing and holding her side.

"What was that for?" I challenged the bird, now safely back on a post and looking at me out of one beady black eye and then another as he turned his head left and right, trying for all his might to look double his size.

"Conk-a-reeee!" he warned, ruffling his feathers.

"He's just protecting his young," Minnie explained. "He thinks you're a predator." I kicked at the dirt, angered and embarrassed, while Minnie retied my hair ribbon, tucking in the hair that came loose in the fray. She let out a stifled giggle and the two of us erupted into sporadic fits of laughter the rest of the way home. That red-winged blackbird followed alongside us half the way home. Persistent devil.

I chuckled at the memory just as the car swerved onto the far side of the road. Chunks of dried dirt pelted the underside of the vehicle as my insides tried to drop through the floor.

"William, wake up!" Minnie screamed.

"Damn!" William exclaimed.

I sat ramrod straight while William grabbed a fierce hold on the wheel and righted us.

"Must have nodded off," he admitted, breathing heavily.

Minnie gave him a wide-eyed stare and held her hand to her chest, calming herself down. "Do you need to take a break?" she asked.

"No, I'll be fine. Just talk to me. The sun is lulling me to sleep."

"That and the fact that you are doing the work of two men, William. Of course you're tired."

The day before, William had loads of chores to do when we got back from the fair. When he finally got in the house well after supper time, Minnie had a plate warming for him on the stove, and he sat with eyes half closed, wolfing it down. He retired to bed soon after without a word to either of us. This was typical of William, however, as he wasn't much of a talker.

"Have you thought any more about getting a hired man, William?" Minnie asked. "You know we can afford it, and there's no sense in working yourself to an early grave."

"I've thought about it," he admitted. "Not sure that I want someone poking around in our business, though. There are things I prefer to keep private."

"We have the separate apartment. It's the perfect thing. I wish you'd agree to it. It's too much work for one man. You could focus your energy on the buying and selling of cattle and let someone else do the chores. Imagine how much more energy you would have!" Minnie had a strong argument, but William wasn't agreeing or disagreeing. He'd fallen into a silence and allowed Minnie to continue her argument for it all the way into DeWitt where we rolled back into a throng of carriages and cars, people dressed in their best for the last day of the fair.

The tragedy of the day before did not seem to dampen the spirits of the people. Most were familiar with death and carrying on in the face of it. Survival continued for those remaining.

One of the boys who knocked me down in the dust the previous day, saw me getting out of the Model T and stuck out his tongue in my general direction. Boys! For the most part, I thought, I'd rather keep my distance. Why'd God have to make them so frustrating?

We strolled past families who had spread out, upon blankets on the ground, picnic lunches of chicken and berry pies, pickles, radishes, cabbage salad, and fresh tomatoes. All of it was enough to make my mouth water and my stomach grumble for its share. "Let's go get something to eat first," Minnie smiled, reading my mind and hearing my stomach's plea.

The food choices were many. Vendors sold brezn with obatzda, a spicy cheese spread. Weisswurst, a white sausage delicacy, pulled in many who had not had the opportunity since the last fair. Brats and sauerkraut were favorites as well. A few couples meandered over to the steckerlfisch, grilled fish on a stick. Almost everyone held onto cups of fresh-squeezed lemonade or mugs of beer.

We waited in line for pulled-pork sandwiches while William and Minnie held separate conversations with acquaintances. The line was slow-moving, and I didn't know a soul. The small town of DeWitt was far enough away from Clinton that not many people from my city bothered to go; Clinton folks were not typically into fairs. That was more of a country thing to do. I watched as girls my age held hands and giggled while making their way over to a large white tent on the other side of the thoroughfare. I recognized it as the same tent in which we watched the boxing demonstration the other day that erupted into disorder when someone's punch landed too hard and fast. Just the same, I was drawn to that place.

"Minnie, can I watch over there while we wait for the food?" I asked, meaning to follow the girls I saw and try to strike up a friendship for a day.

"Go on," she agreed, temporarily distracted by her conversation with a large woman in an ugly brown hat that reared up in back with a plume of purple feathers. The woman's belly protruded over a black belt that was about ready to burst with the effort. While Minnie went back to discussing yesterday's tragedy with the woman, I sprinted off to the tent across the way. I could barely make it inside the flap, there were so many people. I gathered that there was a fight but couldn't see a thing. The girls disappeared into the crowd, so I crouched down low and worked my way under elbows and handbags in an attempt to find them. I broke out in front of the throng only to come within feet of the elevated ring in which the fight broke out the day before. Inside were two fighting men. They circled one another with looks to kill, as Mama always said. Each time a swing met its mark, men and women alike cheered. I saw the girls just ten feet away from me; they stood in front of the adults for a clear view of the action.

Both men were shirtless and shoeless. They hopped about and looked for just the right opening to land the blow that they hoped would end the match. One man had fire-red hair that stuck out over his ears and fanned down his neck. Sweat slipped off the back of his head and down his back. He glistened with effort and let himself hunch over, winded and desperate for an end to the fight. Determined that the end be in his favor, he launched a blow at the other man's jaw.

The punch was perfect, and the other man gritted his teeth. He was slightly overweight but intimidating nonetheless. His fists were as large as meat hooks. Instead of holding his hands up in front of his face, which any school boy or girl knows you'd better do unless you want a sock square in the block, he trudged along with effort and hung his arms at his sides. Clearly this fight had been going on for quite some time. He was winded and careless.

I made my way over to the girls; their eyes were on the red–haired man who appeared as if he was taking control of the situation, pummeling Meat-Hooks with everything he had left in him. "Hi," I tried out my voice in the barrage of shouts surrounding us. The blond one furrowed her brows at me, but her glance went quickly back to the fight as Red wound up his last punch and planted the big guy on the floor with a giant rumble that shook the ground under my feet.

The girls cheered beside me and drowned out my further attempts at temporary friendship. I noticed by now that the other girl had a red tinge to her hair as well, and the same hawk-like look that the victor wore in the ring. She must have been his sister.

"They'll give him an hour's break now," the red girl shouted above the crowd. "Then we'll have the final match!" Although she hadn't so much as acknowledged me, she punctuated her statement with a swing of her fist in my general direction.

"Who'll he fight?" I asked above the roar.

"Who? Don't you know?" asked the blond one. "Everybody knows!"

I shook my head, but didn't say a word.

"The one-armed man!" they both said in unison and sprinted off back into the now slowly-dispersing crowd, leaving me on my own again.

"A one-armed man?" I thought. "They've got to be fooling!"

I found out differently, soon enough.

The fading crowd allowed me an easy path back out to the sandwich and lemonade awaiting me. William and Minnie stood together now and both talked to an older couple I recognized from the Elvira area. They lived over by my brother John. John and the man helped one another during thrashing season, and I'd been present for two or three of the woman's berry pies that were heavenly.

"Well, if it isn't Elsie!" the woman greeted me.

"Hello, maam," I replied.

Minnie asked, "What did you see in there, Elsie?"

"The end of a boxing match!" I got excited thinking about the one upcoming. "And they say the next one is in an hour... a one-armed man will fight!"

"You're kidding!" Minnie laughed.

"She's right," the man corrected her. "I saw him box earlier today. He's quick and accurate. Don't waste any energy on useless punches. Don't see that he'll be able to hold his own in the championship bout, though. Red Walsh ought to be able to keep him at bay."

"Who is he?" Minnie asked.

"Someone said they saw him cleaning up the fair last night. Guess he travels with the fair people. He's one feisty son of a... "

"Harold!" His wife cut him off and gestured in my general direction. "We'll see you two later." She steered him away with a smirk at Minnie.

Harold smirked and cuffed my chin, then tipped his hat at William and Minnie.

Minnie led us over to a set of chairs where we finished our lunch and watched people go by for a little while. Mothers pushed carriages and napping babies, men smoked pipes and cigars; blue smoke danced around Sunday hats.

When done with our lunch, William excused himself and made his way over to a group of men who gestured toward the boxing tent, evidently discussing the upcoming fight. People were already making their way into the tent. William disappeared into the throng. Most of the folks streaming in were men, although the occasional lady poked her way into the flaps of the tent. Children scrambled underneath the sides to avoid the crowds, and I caught a glimpse of the girl with the red hair and her friend.

"Want to?" Minnie asked.

"Sure!" I had a strong curiosity about this one-armed man. If he had made his way to this point in the tournament, he must have been feisty, indeed.

Minnie and I were early enough to be able to stand right up close to the ring at the rear of the tent. People followed us so closely, however, that we couldn't have changed position if we wanted to — we were sandwiched in to stay. William stood opposite us, oblivious to our presence; he stood among his friends and occasionally nodded his head in agreement with something said.

The heat inside the tent was nearly unbearable, and after another 15 minutes, it was totally packed with onlookers. The tent flaps were widened and the sides propped up with poles to let in what breeze existed on a hot, humid Iowa day. The crowd didn't stop coming; people circled the outside of the tent as well.

I took hold of Minnie's hand so as not to get lost in the crowded sea of blood-thirsty spectators. My stomach flipped in on itself in excitement. The hum of conversation surrounding us changed to shouts and words of encouragement for one of the participants, now being led from the rear of the tent up to the ring. The crowd shifted around us to let in Red Walsh, the man I saw fight and win an hour ago. Two fair officials encouraged the crowd to move aside, and he passed just feet from where Minnie and I were standing. His fiery hair had been doused in water and stuck up wildly in all directions. He stepped into the ring and began to shadow box from his corner. He looked like devil spawn with his beaklike nose and burning eyes. Although several people in the crowd shouted encouragement, Red acknowledged no one except the one-armed man now being led through the same path from the back of the tent. His eyes remained intent upon his prey.

The crowd quieted some when the one-armed fighter came in; this man was a stranger to all of us, and a curiosity. It wasn't so much his missing limb that made him a wonder. There were plenty of folks around who'd lost fingers, toes, and limbs in wagon accidents and lumber mills. It was his ability to whoop all those men before him. To get to this point in the boxing tournament, he'd beaten a total of ten men — no small feat in a pool of men and boys who'd learned the trade from the likes of Bill Burnham. Burnham went out East and won himself a world championship at the age of 22, then came back to Iowa to start boxing clubs throughout Clinton and Scott counties. Burnham was dead now, but his boxing progeny dotted the crowd and carried a torch for the only one left who'd learned the art of fighting from the one man who'd made our corner of the world famous. Red Walsh was our last hope. Whoever this one-armed wonder was, surely he couldn't beat the best of the Burnham clubs.

Calm and cool as a summer cucumber, the one-armed man threaded his way through our stares. His olive arm brushed up against my best white dress, sending a thrill through my spine that balanced me up on my toes in anticipation. His well-toned back, slick with sweat, ducked underneath the lowest rope. The left arm was the one missing. Its presence was now reduced to a stump that dangled five or so inches from his shoulder and ended in a mass of red scar tissue, but it was his right side that drew my attention and caused a few women in the crowd to gasp. The muscles on the right arm more than made up for the absence of any on the left side. His arm was a marvel. Its form and strength were impressive, to be sure. I wondered what it might be like to run my hand over it, to feel the veins popping from its surface.

His hair was jet black and fell over his dark eyes in wisps that had the curious effect of allowing him to see out but never letting the onlooker feel as if she knew her way in. His chest rose and fell with strong, deep breaths that showed his calm resolve.

He looked upon the raging Red Walsh with a slight grin that only served to make Red even fierier.

Mr. Matthias Stark, the pudgy and heaving fair marshall, held up his arms to quiet the crowd, exposing the half moons of sweat brimming on his white shirt. He dabbed a black tie to his forehead and managed a smile at the crowd as they followed his gestured instructions.

"Gentlemen . . . and ladies," he nodded to Minnie and the other women who dared enter the tent, "welcome to the championship match!" Hoorays broke out among the crowd, but quickly died in favor of getting the match started. "To my left you have our local and accomplished Red Walsh!"

More hoorays from the crowd and a shout from the red-haired sister, "Go, Red!"

Money changed hands everywhere. William gestured at the one-armed man. He'd chosen him as champion and was willing to bet on it.

"And to my right," Mr. Stark continued, "is the traveling man — Marcel Masters!"

Murmurs of appreciation and anticipation rippled through the crowd as everyone could taste the excitement. I wasn't sure whom I would have put my money on at that moment. I'd seen Red fight, and knew him to be skilled and confident, but something about Marcel Masters and his calm assuredness made me unsure of Red's chances to overtake him.

Perhaps Red would be too confident in his ability to dominate one who so clearly had a disadvantage. Perhaps every disadvantage can be turned otherwise.

"May the best man win!" Stark concluded and nodded to an elderly man with a bell down on the floor. The referee exchanged places with the Fair Marshall who heaved his large body underneath the ropes while two men helped him down. The elderly man grinned heartily and struck the bell. And so it began.

Red started to bounce from left to right, sizing up this dark, calm thing across from him. Marcel circled, his right fist in front of his face, and forced Red to turn round and round to follow him, lest his back be turned.

"Patience, Red!" a man from the crowd shouted. Red Walsh grinned then, willing to continue this dance and learn what his opponent was capable of. Marcel however, was fully self-possessed and needed no reminders. There seemed to be no one in his corner, besides. They circled one another for a full minute before Red's impatience was revealed by side-to-side motions of his head and precarious teasing jabs at his opponent's face. Red curled his lip up slightly and looked menacing for a second, but his countenance changed as soon as his opponent muttered a few words, unheard by the crowd.

Whatever was said, Red's eyes bulged big as Mama's saucers and he lodged a haymaker at Marcel's face. The man had no problem dodging the blow; everyone could see it coming for miles. The crowd exploded with encouragement for the hometown boy. No one knew this one-armed man. Despite our hope, it didn't take long for us all to realize that we were watching something akin to a bout between a cat and a wounded mouse. Only Marcel Masters wasn't the wounded mouse.

Red's lost haymaker only made him angrier. The heat rose on his skin until it nearly matched his hair, flaming and bright. He showed a little more caution now, wary that he launch another failed blow. Then Marcel did a curious thing. He turned his back on him. Poor Red didn't know what to do at that point; surely no one had ever done that in a bout against him before. He tried to jostle around to the front of him to gauge what the heck was going on, but Marcel just continued to sidle round and round so as to keep Red at his back. The flames really rose on Red's face then; his ears seemed about fit to burn off his head, for he was sure that this strange man was making fun of him. He began to shout, "Turn back around, freak! Turn back around and fight!"

And with a lightning flash of determination, Marcel did turn back around. A bullet of muscle and pain landed right on Red's yammering jaw and shut him up well enough.

The roaring of the crowd died down to a dull shock just before Red's defeated frame landed on the floor with a horrible thud. The referee counted to ten, and that was all she wrote, so to speak.

The next sounds were those of Red's family and friends who clambered into the ring to check on their overtaken champion. Marcel betrayed no emotion, just looked around at the shocked crowd and let himself down near Minnie and me. He surely didn't notice us at all in that moment, just flowed down the same path he came in on, the silent crowd parting and staring at the marvel who beat the best we had to offer.

Several men handed William his winnings. He was one of only a few who had been willing to bet against Red. By the time he collected it all, William had a fat roll of bills that he tucked into his jacket pocket.

Red came around eventually; cold water in the face will do that to you, but by the time he did so, most of the crowd had dispersed and made their way to the next distraction. The auto races were about to begin.

As Minnie and I were up against the ring itself, we were among some of the last people to leave the tent. We'd lost sight of William in the crowd, and when we broke free of the canvas, we spent some time looking around for him.

"Oh, he's probably made his way to the beer tent!" Minnie joked. But just as she said so, I pulled on her sleeve and pointed down the side of the boxing tent. William stood with the one-armed man, congratulating him on his win.

We walked down to join them and had just about made our way there, when a tall, blond man in a suit coat and tie, huffed around the back corner and made a beeline straight for Marcel.

"Masters! I need to talk to you!" the man ordered. "Excuse us," he apologized to William, tipping his hat slightly.

While Marcel made his way over to the angry man, William walked the ten or so feet over to Minnie and me. We discussed going to see the auto races and paid the talk between the two men no mind, until the conversation wasn't a conversation anymore. The man began to shout.

"It's not good for business!" he screamed.

"If you paid me more, I might have a care for your business."

"We're all in this together, Marcel, you know that."

"This is just a job to me, Max. I'm not one of you people."

"You've got a helluva lot of nerve after all I've done for you." The blond man pulled the hat off his head, hitting it on his leg.

"I never asked it of you. Like I said, I'm *not* one of you people."

"Well, I guess this is your last stop then, Marcel. If you're not going to be good for business, you're not going to be part of the business." The man turned and stalked away.

William told Minnie and me to go ahead to the races; he'd meet us there. It wasn't until after the races were over and we were getting into William's car, that we were told of our extra passenger.

The sun set on the dusty fairgrounds, all manner of young and old retreated to carriages and Fords or walked back to local residences. Children slept in the arms of their fathers. Sassy teenagers held onto the last minutes together, laughing between the tents and sneaking sips of the now-warm beer.

I sat in the back of the car, head against the side, sleepy and sweaty, while William and Minnie talked in low tones outside.

"William, we don't even know him!" Minnie said.

"You wanted me to get a hired man, now we have one."

"But not some stranger… surely there's someone around Elvira who could do the job just as well."

"Not that I know of. McCullough's boys are all needed at home. Walter isn't old enough yet. Thomson's not reliable. There's not that many to choose from."

"Well, you might be right about that," Minnie admitted. "Still… how much work do you think he'll be able to do in the condition that he's in?"

"I suspect he'll be able to hold his own better than you know. You saw him in the ring today."

Marcel Masters walked over the grass on his way to us. He'd a small satchel over his shoulder and held a soft parcel under his arm. He peered at Minnie and William from under his long, black hair.

William introduced him to Minnie. Marcel nodded his head. Next thing I knew he slid next to me and asked, "How do you do?"

William had his hired man.

October 1905

William is mostly soft and loving, with a few hard edges that take him out to the barn when he doesn't understand me or know what to say. Better to flee than confront the parts of me he doesn't like. For one, he wonders at my indecisiveness. Bacon or sausage for breakfast? My pale blue dress or the yellow one for today? In the front door or the back? Hang this shirt up on the line first, or that one? A stitch here or there? Sometimes the tiniest increments and seemingly inconsequential decisions feel as if the weight of the world relies upon them.

If I wear the yellow dress it will be a bright, cheery day. The blue one will bring melancholy. Go in the same door I went out or bad luck will befall me or someone I love. A stitch in just the right place will tidy up the day, there, and I won't be able to fall asleep tonight. Do others have such thoughts? It all feels so real. I don't dare voice these ideas. Just tuck them away and hide them under handkerchiefs in a tobacco box. These thoughts, like mindless chickens, sense danger where no danger lurks, but force and bend me to their making when the moment strikes — a rape of will.

January 1906

It was so wonderful to see my family for the holidays. I can't wait to have a big family of my own, so I don't have to wait for special occasions to experience the glow of a large, happy family. I have felt the ache of missing home for so many months now.

The new quilt Mama gave me for Christmas adorns the sofa in the sitting room. It feels so much cozier in there now! Somehow the never-ending sewing and mending I must do doesn't seem so bad when I have her quilt around me.

Everything feels warmer and cheerier today. Even the scraggly red cedar trees in the ditches look pretty with the new fallen snow clinging to them.

Soon we'll be heading out to Schroeder's pond for ice skating. It certainly is frozen right through with the winter we have been having! We could probably skate right along Brophy Creek to get there. Patty has offered hot chocolate back at her house when we are all done to keep us warm on the ride home. I'm sure I'll be snuggled up with my quilt when we get back!

I need an outing. We don't get out and DO things nearly as often as people do in Clinton. After all, there isn't much TO do.

Memory

Look back at all the important moments.
What can you recall that may be meaningful?

The morning dawned hotter than words can fully express. Deep penetrating hot like Mama's kitchen at noon. It was sweet corn Saturday, and it only came once a year. I stood out in the ditch. My job was to catch the ears as they sailed over the tall stalks of corn. My Mama, Minnie, Nell, Mary, and Melinda were somewhere in the field picking and chucking, picking and chucking, with only me to pick it up. I didn't complain. My job was far better. Despite the heat, all the women donned men's long pants, long-sleeved shirts, work boots, and handkerchiefs over their heads to protect them from the sharp blades of corn, insects — mosquitoes, flies, gnats, and the like — and the relentless sun. I danced about from fallen ear to fallen ear in my summer day dress that rose and fell with my bouncing strides to and from the corn we would later shuck, shave, and boil for our root cellars. Occasionally the ears pelted me but not hard enough to do any damage. The only one with any strength was Mama, and she couldn't throw something straight to save her life.

From my filled gunnysack, I emptied the ears into a wagon that sat waiting on the road. Earlier that morning, before I was even awake, John drove it out there to receive the hoards of sweet corn that we would harvest that day. When I first looked at the large, empty wagon, I wondered how we would ever fill it. I thought we'd work forever and a day. But Mama said we'd pick until the wagon was full, and she wasn't kidding. Pick and chuck, pick and chuck, all darn morning.

Just when hunger nearly struck me down for dead, the women finally emerged from the sweet corn patch. I hadn't seen them for hours. They looked like other creatures entirely. The near noon sun beat down on our tired heads and they emerged, soaked with sweat. Mama looked like a portly man coming from the patch in her men's pants. They must have been big John's, for they weren't my father's. Her hips were twice the size of his. Minnie emerged, white as a ghost. "Lord, Mama! Look at Minnie!" I exclaimed, just as her legs went limp right under her, and she slumped down into the tall grass like a lanky foal. We all rushed to her.

"She's just over-hot is all. She needs cooling off and some water," Mary proclaimed. Minnie babbled something incoherent and shook her head. Her face shone pale white despite the morning sun. We shielded her from its relentless rays with our bodies, and after a few minutes and some water she was ready to be back on her feet.

"I'm fine. I'm fine," Minnie assured us.

John came down the road with the horse and cart to pull the wagon back to his place. He assessed the situation with his goofy gaze. "Hop in!" John encouraged. "I'll take you for a dip before we head back. You gals look fit for nothing!" He jumped out of his seat and helped each one of us into the wagon. Mama got in the seat next to him up front. The rest of us sat atop the corn in the back, precarious, but better than walking. He took special care with Minnie, after being told that she just recently fainted away in the heat. "You all hang on now, and you'll be cooled off in no time!"

As John pulled right up to the pond in back of his farmhouse, he jumped down and jogged over to where I sat. He hauled me out screaming and giggling and tossed me right in the water.

"Sakes, John!" Mama scolded, lumbering out of the wagon. "She's getting a bit old for such nonsense!"

"Ah, Mama," John waved her off. "You're never too old for a little bit of play!" John splashed at her, covering Mama's whole front side. Before she could utter a protest, John slipped and fell backward in the water. All of us, even Mama, laughed at his foolery. John chuckled right alongside us while clambering for the shore.

After stripping down to her underthings, Minnie waded out as far as she could go and floated on her back. I couldn't resist and went right out there with her. From across the pond I heard something plop back into the water. "Probably a big old snapping turtle," I thought. As I lay on my back alongside Minnie, I imagined that cranky turtle coming over by me and clamping his strong jaws down on my big toe. Sometimes my imagination took me over, like right then. I tried not to look frightened but hightailed it back to shore.

Nell, Mary, and Mama all stood at the pond's edge; they used their handkerchiefs to soak up water and squeeze it onto their necks and heads. Nell's pants were rolled up to her knees, and she stood barefoot squeezing her toes through the soft mud. Feeling playful she scrunched up some mud between her toes and flung it at John who reclined on the bank.

I joined in with a splash in his general direction. My aim, however, was quite off, and I doused Mama instead.

That was enough fooling around for Mama, and she declared it was time to get back to work. "All right now, let's go. We've got a full day's work ahead of us and not a full day to do it."

I trudged back into the wagon, and John drove us all a mile and a half to Minnie's place where the second stage of the day was to take place. The end result of all this hard work was to be canned corn, enough to feed our four families for the year and beyond, most likely. I thought we had enough corn to feed the county 'til doomsday.

Minnie's place was quiet when we got back. Both William and Marcel were out checking cattle and fence lines. John pulled the wagon up alongside the pigpen where we would throw the husks and cobs for the hogs. As soon as the wagon was unhitched, we said our goodbyes to him. John had plenty of work to do back at his own place.

"Thanks for the dip in the pond, John. I needed that!" Minnie said.

"You looked like you could use a cooling off, sister!" John replied. "Besides, you know I'd do anything for you!"

"I do, big brother… I do."

And we all knew that was the truth. Family was everything to John. Always had been.

Most of our community was German back then, but there were plenty of exceptions. People from England, France, Poland, Holland, and even Italy dotted the countryside. Most folks were first or second generation to the area, (Mama and Papa arrived there in the 1880s) so they brought along all their old bitterness and rivalry to the new country. In other words, they pretty much stuck with their own kind. Whatever that meant. It never did make much sense to me, but that's the way things were back then. The German people like us gathered on Friday nights for barn dances. A variety of instruments played, trumpets and trombones, drums, the occasional guitar, and the ubiquitous accordion. That was my favorite — the accordion. I loved to spell it in German. Akkordeon, akkordeon, akkordeon. Have you ever had a favorite word? Like ubiquitous, for example. That's my new favorite word because it can mean so many strange and mysterious things. My old favorite word was *akkordeon*. I suppose that's because John played it, and played it well. I knelt mesmerized at the light and intricate work of his big fingers. They didn't look capable of such a dance. Whenever our family gathered, John took me out underneath the trees and taught me the breath of the accordion and how to feel the life within. That was the first thing I had to learn. Once I could appreciate the basic nature of it, John taught me to make it dance. Mine though, was a clumsy child tune, and John knew the most marvelous songs from the Old Country.

Before my bigger brothers and sisters were old enough to help out around Mama and Papa's hotel, they were sent off to attend school. Minnie and John were closest in age and ended up in the same classroom in Clinton. Those ages 6-8 were taught by Miss Welling, whom I did not have the *displeasure* of having. Minnie and John shared stories of her many a time around the dinner table. One story in particular seemed to bring them closer together each time they told it. John was 8 at the time and had already been in school for two years. Minnie was new and just arrived at age 6.

Those of all backgrounds attended Miss Welling's class, and at any one time, five languages could be heard uttered out on the playground. During class time the only language allowed was English, and any student who tried to pull one over on Miss Welling could be sent to a round with the stick and the coal chores. She was set against German and Italian for sure, and if she heard them in her classroom, she was certain that some obscenities were being uttered. Miss Welling herself was English and impatient with languages she couldn't speak herself. This attitude trickled down to the non-German and non-Italian children, creating a tone of intolerance throughout the whole classroom.

Minnie was not quick to pick up the English language. After all, Mama and Papa did not speak it themselves until years later. As a small child, the only language she ever heard spoken at home was German. By the time I came along, Papa believed it was prudent to learn the language for the sake of business and painstakingly did so. Most of what he picked up came from my older brothers and sisters through what they learned at school. Papa read voraciously in German and reluctantly in English, but he could speak it as well as we could after a time. Mama, however, was another story.

Back when Minnie was little, though, she was not a master of this new language. School came difficult for her only for this reason. She was sharp in mathematics and the German language. She had knowledge of music and was okay with people, but she did not pick up on the demands of Miss Welling until she was able to look at her classmates for direction.

Miss Welling stood at the board, chalk in hand and a simple mathematics problem poised and ready for solution. One that Minnie could have solved in her sleep. But instead of calling her name as any kind and caring teacher would, Miss Welling said with her back turned to the class, "The little German girl in the back, come up here and try to solve this one." Well, of course, Minnie had no idea what she said, so sat there, staring and waiting for some cue. What she got was a classroom of kids staring at her and Miss Welling's impatient gaze. By the time Minnie realized what she was supposed to do, a chorus of shouts and protruding tongues came from the students around her and she was much too embarrassed and upset to solve anything. Instead of walking up to the board, Minnie ran from the room and Miss Welling moved on to her next victim. John slipped out undetected, to find her. They sat together underneath the oak trees where Minnie cried and John held her and patted her head the way he'd seen Papa do so many times before. They were both softies for Minnie and the rest of the sisters.

When the class came out for recess with the only rubber ball the school owned, Zachariah Webb, surrounded by his cronies and poised for trouble, launched the ball straight at Minnie's head. The ball struck her without warning and bounced off. John did not hesitate. His brown shoes kicked up dust as he ran over to a surprised Zachariah and launched a perfect blow right at his face. A trickle of blood oozed out of Zachariah's nose, and for a second everyone was quiet. Then, like a couple of tomcats in a bag, John and Zachariah went at it with the whole class surrounding them and shouting.

Minnie stood up and saw Miss Welling on the school steps, arms crossed. She may have been mistaken, but Minnie said she saw a slight smile on Miss Welling's face, which could have been the case, for Miss Welling made no move to break up the fight.

Zachariah Webb was a big boy, English, and a class bully if there ever was one. He was also Miss Welling's class pet. She probably figured he could take care of himself. Well, that thought needed some revision. For if there's one thing that matters, it's family. And no matter what John's general demeanor (he was usually pretty light-hearted and fun) family honor was at stake. The spring calf was now a hardened bull. Zachariah was able to land a punch to his face and rip John's only school shirt, but John soon landed another punch to Zachariah's already tender nose, which landed him on his rump. My brother descended like a red hawk on its prey, knocked Zachariah flat on his back, and proceeded to pummel him silly. As soon as Zachariah was on his back and it was clear the fight was over, the students quieted down, expecting John to stop. He didn't. There were no sounds coming out of Zachariah Webb, save the labored breathing of one with blood oozing from his nose. And there were the horrid sounds of quick knuckles on bony flesh.

Minnie emerged slowly through the crowd and placed a hand on John's shoulder. She managed to say, in German, "Stop, John." With another punch to the face for good measure and assertion, John stood, winded and fierce. He proclaimed proudly, in German, and in Miss Welling's general direction, "Let that be a lesson to you bastards!" The class moved aside then, certain that Miss Welling would choose to descend with her stick at that point. She didn't.

"John Edens, you are done here. I'll not have you in my classroom. Wilhelmina, you may come back when you have composed yourself and can follow directions. Go!" Miss Welling demanded, pointing in the general direction of our home.

John took Minnie's hand then. He gave each of his classmates a stare for good measure, and spat in the direction of his now former teacher. They walked off in silence, for home.

That was the end of John's school days. Mama and Papa allowed

Minnie to return a year later, when Miss Welling moved on and was replaced by the much beloved and respected Miss Schroeder.

That was the kind of brother John was to us all. If a hard thing needed doing, then it was John we all went to for help. Even Mama and Papa learned this through the years and solicited his help when the occasional filcher made his way into the hotel and needed kicking out. He was a good laugh until someone decided to wrong his family. Then look out, world!

John left us then, back for home. On his way out he passed Marcel striding in from the field and touched his hat in greeting. Marcel did the same and walked over. I think we were all a bit overwhelmed by the mountain of work ahead of us. Even Mama stared in dismay at the pile of corn that needed shucking.

"Looks like you gals have a lot of work ahead of you! How 'bout I help you get started?" Marcel broke the mood and we all welcomed the extra hand in tackling the hundreds of ears ahead of us. He hauled over a stump to sit on and got right to work.

I couldn't help staring at him. Marcel was quicker than all of us, save Mama, at stripping the ears of their protective layer. Using his knees to keep the corn still, he worked that ear with his one hand until there was nothing left save golden, shiny kernels.

I was practically useless at the job. Every ear I threw in the "done" pile Mama fished out and tossed back at me. "There's still hair on that one! Be careful!" she scolded. I looked at all the silk clinging and sticky and gave up before I even got started. That job seemed hopeless, and I longed for another task to no immediate avail.

"So, Marcel," Mary asked, "Minnie tells us you're good help around here. Seems you're just as fit with one arm as most men are with two."

"I try to be," Marcel replied. "I've had plenty of practice."

"If you don't mind my asking, how did it happen?" Mary asked.

Marcel's eyes darkened just then, although I'm sure I'm the only one who saw it. Despite the conversation, all eyes were on the work at hand, save mine.

"You know, ladies… I'd better be off to finish my chores. It'll be noon soon, and I've plenty to do before lunch." Marcel walked off in the direction of the barn. He left a half-done ear of corn on the stump.

"I suppose I shouldn't have asked that."

"It's seems a sore subject with him… best not ask again, " Minnie warned.

"It must be getting close to noon by now. Minnie, you could use some time out of the sun. You're looking a bit peaked again. Why don't you go on in and fix us noon dinner? We'll finish up here," Mama decided.

I looked at Mama longingly. Without a word, Mama read my mind. "Oh, for heaven sakes, go with her and help! You're not any good out here, anyway!"

Once inside, Minnie and I began lunch for eight. The ladies would eat along with William and Marcel who'd be back for the meal as well. I began boiling a pot for the potatoes and got to work peeling, while Minnie prepared the liver and onions. I didn't have the heart to say a thing, but liver and onions had to be the worst meal I could ever imagine. Mama usually served it once a week, and it was all I could do to choke it down. I didn't dare complain about it, though. If I did, Mama would have boxed my ears for sure. You just didn't complain about food in my family. Like as not, you'd end up with nothing if you did. Something was better than nothing, in theory. My mouth didn't think so, though, nor my nose. As far as I knew, I was the only one in my family who didn't like it. Minnie served it just as often as Mama did.

Minnie must have been sick then, I thought, for when the potatoes were boiling and the liver and onions were frying in the pan, her pale face turned green.

"Are you all right, Minnie?" I asked.

Minnie answered with a retreat out the front door. When I followed, I heard her retching over the fence.

Mama approached her with a smile. Unusual, I thought, considering the situation. Minnie was clearly ill. "I thought so this morning when you fainted, Minnie. Now I know. You're with child, girl."

I stopped in my tracks.

Minnie stood and dabbed her mouth with a handerchief. "That's what it is? Is it? I suppose so!"

February 1906

The February blues have set in. The roads remain impassable. The only way we could get to Clinton is with snowshoes! Thank goodness I've finally gotten used to planning ahead. We have plenty of supplies for another two weeks at least. We can only get so much here in Elvira. The local store has basic supplies but nothing like home.

I've gone stir crazy in the house. William has too, I think. The cabin fever has set in. I've taken to long moments staring out the window while William finds reasons to be angry. Not with me ... but at little things — objects. He can't stand to sit still for very long, and with nowhere to go, he doesn't have much choice. He's taken to long periods of time in the barns, fussing over this and that. Things that I'm sure don't need doing; he can't help but find some excuse to leave the house.

My excuse comes tomorrow night. The ladies of Zion Lutheran are holding a rag-rug social. We're all to bring our old worn clothes and such and the older women will show us how to make use of them by somehow sewing strips of old rags together. Anything to get out of the house!

As soon as the roads clear, I'm talking William into coming to town. The first thing I'll do is get the ingredients for Glühwein. I think only Mama's mulled wine will cure my blues and this dreadful feeling of cold that has settled over me!

April 1906

Finally, some excitement around here! Two natives traveled through Elvira today. I saw them on the way to the store and met them there as well. Both were males and led shaggy ponies laden with furs. I forgot all manners and couldn't help but watch them as much as I dared. The men exchanged furs for material, flour, coffee, and salt. They smelled of cedar and far winds. Their strangeness — a sunny day. I can smell spring taunting me.

After they were on their way, the talk in the store was of history. Apparently this town was called Pleasant Prairie back in 1840. Indians burned the place to the ground. The survivors picked up their skirts and relocated, like chickens, to a spot just as precarious, just a shade more to the east and farther away from the creek. I wonder, where are all the Indians now?

Spring was here
The wind first blew it in
Then the birds came
Loud as thunderous night
Oddball species from far south and east
Brought in waves of vibrations
Perched in lilacs and plum trees
And called to us
New ideas
New feelings
New possibilities

The blood. I remember the blood. Screams of pain. Mama's reassuring murmurs to Minnie and scolding to me when I couldn't move fast enough.

"Hurry! Tie the center of the rope in a knot. Hurry!"

"I've got it!" I assured her, and flung it to her outstretched hand.

"Repeat after me, Minnie. I don't care how hurt you are. You can do this!"

Mama placed the knotted rope in her oldest daughter's hands, made slippery with Minnie's own blood, and directed the cadence. "As this knot holds firm, so you hold firm in my womb. As this knot holds firm, so you hold firm in my womb."

Minnie grimaced, "As this knot holds firm … "

* * * * *

They tried to conceive for many years. William remained anxious for a son, someone to help with the vast tracks of land and the cattle that grazed upon it. Someone to carry on the family name.

Minnie didn't care for the gender of the child, only that it be hers to keep and raise. When years passed and no child came, Mama told her to write to our aunts in the Old Country. Mama knew some things about birthing and keeping babies. She knew her sisters in Germany held onto some ancient tricks to make babies come.

Aunt Adelinde's package arrived on the 13th. Just two days earlier could have made all the difference. The 11th is a lucky day. Happy things start on the 11th. It's not lucky to begin things on the 13th. You'll see.

Dearest Niece,

Plant basil, parsley, and lemon balm for tea.
Seeds enclosed.
Eat flies from the windowsills.
Most importantly,
Stay away from all cemeteries and scenes of death.
When baby comes, bathe it in birthing blood for long life.

Love and The Lord's blessings from Germany!

* * * * *

Minnie steeped teas and snatched flies by night and day. And so the event eventually came to pass — a baby grew inside her.

Though Minnie lived near Elvira, ten miles away, we felt like neighbors. William taught her to drive his new automobile — one of the first in Clinton County. Occasionally she would pick me up for a drive around town or a jaunt out to their farm. Certainly she was the only woman behind the helm of an automobile. Minnie received many stares from passersby. She simply smiled and waved back at them. "I am a sight, aren't I?" she'd ask me.

"Helllllllooooooo!" Minnie called from our front door. "I'm wondering if an Elsie Edens would like to come with me to the store today!"

I tore from the kitchen, dishtowel in hand, and Mama scowled behind me.

"Some of us have better things to do than run off to the store!" Mama scolded.

"Oh, Mama, give her a break. She's only a girl yet. Besides, I'd like to take her back to Elvira with me afterward. I could use her help around the house for a few days, with the baby coming and all."

The promise of work and not idleness for me was the ticket for Mama. She'd been telling Minnie "Don't lift this and that," for a month now. I was to be of some use.

Minnie chose a dress pattern and material from Van Allen's Department Store. No more tightly buttoned skirts and tucked waists. Minnie took tips from Jeannie Watt and her German pro-dress reform handbook. Dresses to grow and breathe in! Errand complete, we drove out to the countryside.

My braids whipped in the wind as we turned onto the dirt road to her home in Elvira. We chatted of baby names and tried to remember the old songs mother sang to us when we were little. I sang one line from an ancient tune, "and down fall pleasant dreams for thee… " as lonely grey tombstones came into view in the countryside graveyard.

Minnie looked at me strangely then, and the automobile crested Cemetery Hill, suddenly revealing the rear of a horse and rider.

"Oh!" I shrieked. In a panic, Minnie cranked the wheel hard right and instead of slamming on the brake, she pressed the gas. I gripped the seats and screamed. Out of the corner of my eye I saw the horse rear up in terror. She clutched her belly as the auto veered into the ditch and beyond, stopping abruptly against a hill in the cemetery. My door wedged so tightly against the earth there was no opening it.

"Are you okay?"

Looking down at her belly, I asked, "Are you?"

"You gals all right down there?" The man on the horse called.

He momentarily distracted Minnie as she opened her door and stepped out unknowingly onto the gravesite of Marcel Theodore Stuedemann 1808-1879. She recoiled when her dress brushed the side of the stone and refused to leave the car.

"I can't leave it!" Minnie cried. "It may be done already! I can't leave it!"

"Stay away from all cemeteries and scenes of death," I remembered and explained the curse to the man. He walked his mount around to the side of the car and gently helped Minnie up onto the horse.

As I clambered out her side of the auto, a solitary portent of blood trickled down Minnie's tan stockings, and tears streamed down her face.

"Get going!" I yelled. "Take her back to Mama!" I struck the horse's haunches with all my might and took off in a run after them.

They say the old gods and superstitions travel over land and sea. Too bad it's not just the good ones.

"As this knot hold firm, so you hold firm in my womb," Mother led, but it was too late.

When Minnie recovered enough to hold the dead infant, she dipped her finger in blood from the sheets and anointed the tiny child with a red cross on its fragile head.

Well, I think the warmth is finally here to stay. After the unpredictable spring weather — snow, rain, wind, rain, snow, wind, wind, rain, wind… the sun has finally decided it's time to shine. Near the creaky windmill I've planted all I can in the one garden — kartoffel, tomato, onion, carrot, beans, peas, turnip. That's one skill Mama taught me that stuck! Come July things will start popping out so fast it will be a full time job to preserve it all. Lord knows I would rather be tending the gardens than the animals.

William has forgotten his goal of turning me into the emergency farmhand. I never did get it right enough for him. I suppose I can't blame him though; the gander gets the best of me, the cow doesn't cooperate when I try to milk her (I get more milk on the floor than in the bucket), and I've forgotten to take care of the hogs more than once. The cattle that William has scattered out and about the countryside I've never had to deal with, thank goodness.

I am proud to say, however, that my book skills have found their place. William is adept at farming and dealing; he can read, but he's not very strong when it comes to bookkeeping. I watched him struggle over sums after dinner one night. His frustration caused him to push the figures away and storm off into the night. When he came back, I'd finished the books, double-checked the figures, and found that William indeed is a shrewd businessman. He knows what he is doing in theory, but he lacks skill with numbers. I've taken it upon myself to organize the receipts from the stock merchants, feed stores, and others. I've also completely taken over the bankbooks.

William was taken aback at first. I know it's not typically a woman's job to do such. It's certainly a weight off his shoulders, though; that much I can tell. I certainly don't mind it. One very nice thing about it is that William will be bringing me to Clinton much more often for bank business, and I will be able to visit my family. William might see fit to teach me to drive after all, so he can stay in the country and take care of things here.

The newest copy of The Ladies Home Journal has not only one, but two advertisements for automobiles with women at the

61

helm. I've strategically placed these open at the dinner table in the hopes that an idea will be planted in William's head.

August 1906

Good news! William has been voted in as the local and newly formed Beef Association president. The Pure Food and Drug Act was passed a few months ago, and many local farmers are concerned with how this might affect their livelihood. Many don't speak good English let alone write and read it, so they don't understand the new laws. William knows the laws, the people, and the cattle business, so he's been determined the best choice to help the locals interpret and carry out their business. William has warned me that due to the new regulations, someday we are doomed to a large-scale loss. It does sound frightening, but I have no doubt William will protect our interests.

Description

Familiarize yourself with the known facts and
be able to write them down. What is fact and
what is opinion?

John and Nell's barn dance commenced with the setting of the sun and an end to the day's work. The whole countryside was ready to play. Noisy musicians poured out of dirty cars and stumbled, already drunk, into the barn to begin a dance that would last until midnight or later. Couples and families arrived via wagon and auto, on horse or on foot to Elvira's best summer party.

Underneath the maple trees, tables overflowed with offerings from each family — brezn and streudels, nuts, rhubarb crisp, cakes, breads with homemade jam, fresh vegetables cut and sliced, cider, cookies, wurstl, and meatballs. Fried hendle drumsticks were picked up hand over fist by a group of little girls who trailed brightly colored hair ribbons. Women squealed at the sight of each other's homemade goods while men clapped one another on the back and looked longingly at the spread.

The music began in the barn with a flourish of warm-ups led by my brother John. He'd played the accordion since age ten. John was taught by the owner of a local "freak show" in Clinton. For a dime, locals, drunks, clam diggers in from the boats, visitors, country people, and kids could see a melancholy, but mysterious group of misfits secreted away and protected by a Mr. Stan Polanski. Rumor had it, he had once been a partner in a major traveling circus. Polanski was charged with a crime of some sort and kicked out of the partnership for good. Several of the circus personnel followed him. Most of the people were exceptional in some rare and awe–inspiring way. These people had run away *from* the circus. Anyway, the owner took a liking to my brother, for John spent quite a few dimes disappearing in the shadows of that place. By the time I was old enough to go by myself, they'd all moved on and the place was taken over by a tobacco merchant. When Stan left, too old to take care of himself, much less anyone else, he sold his accordion to my brother for $1.

That same accordion led the pack of trumpets, clarinets, and trombones blasting out polkas and waltzes to entertain the crowd. As usual, the little ones were the first to dance. Soon they would be asleep in parked cars or on blankets in the grass, and the adults would take over the dance floor.

We served dinner and mugs of cold beer at Mama and Papa's hotel, The Farmer's Home. So named because of all the farmers who went one way and another across the Mississippi or along it, for business. The dark brown liquid never appealed to me; it always smelled a little sour when left behind on stools and floors overnight, and the way it combined with the cigar smoke nearly choked me out. That night there was something altogether different about the thought of it, home-brewed by my brother and served under the chorus of crickets serenading me. All felt magical, something awake and alive, apart from city life and wonderful. So when Tolly Tompkins called me over to have a sip of the one glass he and some others had secreted from the adults, I took him up on it.

He led me and a group of dirty boys to a spot behind John's barn. The sharp smell of fresh cut hay surrounded us as we perched on top of the bales and gazed upward at the stars.

With giggles and spurts, the boys passed the cup around to each other, taking small sips. Last in line, I decided to show the boys how grown up city girls could be.

"Don't drink too much," Tolly warned, "It'll make you drunk!"

"I've been around this stuff for ages," I boasted. "Isn't any big deal at all . . . In fact, it quenches the thirst!" With a flourish, I brought the mug up to my lips and drained the rest of the cup.

"Damn! Whadja do that for? Now there's no more for us!" Tolly admonished, partly impressed, but angry.

I wiped the foam from my lips and smiled at him. Then I handed over the cup and walked off toward the barn. "Thanks for the beer, Tolly!" I whispered over my shoulder, feeling sassy and slightly guilty at the same time.

I wandered in and out of John's outbuildings, not quite ready to return to the party. I startled a group of sleeping chickens in the chicken house, and was surprised myself when a slinking cat met me around a corner.

One end of John's cattle shed lay bare and open in the moonlight; a couple tumbled down into fresh-laid hay. The horses shifted in their stalls, and one let out a small nicker of protest. I heard the woman mumble while the man shushed her. I longed to see who it was and what exactly they were doing. That mumble sounded familiar to me, but I didn't know too many from this area, just my sisters and a few of their older friends. I heard the woman exclaim, "Stop it now … we need to get back!" There seemed an urgency to the woman's voice. I got out of there before someone thought I was spying.

Mama and Papa planned to leave early that night, and I was to stay with Minnie and William, so I had the whole evening ahead of me yet and lots of potential mischief to get into. The beer went straight to my head and caused me to feel a bit bolder than usual. I sauntered into the barn where John and his friends played my favorite dance — the polka! Parents stood around the dance floor watching frolicking young ones. Men played cards in the corners and threw poker chips while sipping beer. A few couples danced together. Tobacco smoke filled the air and mingled with the sweet smell of fresh hay strewn about the floor. I wove my way through the people and waved at Minnie, who stood talking to a group of women just inside the door. She smoothed her long sandy-blond hair that she'd allowed to hang loose for to-night's dance. Quite unorthodox for a woman at the time, most ladies wound their hair in tight buns and wore hats whenever going outside the house. Minnie however, did not believe in such norms. She wore her hair as God Himself gave it to her. She appeared distracted, but smiled at me as I stomped round on the dirt floor with the little kids kicking up plumes of dust from the hard-packed earth. A little boy and girl, not more than three, dirty and smiling, held hands and spun round and round.

I have to admit that the jigging around, combined with the glass of beer, made me feel a bit woozy. I'd been dancing for over and hour, my forehead burst with sweat, and things started to go a bit starry, so I decided it was time to go out for some air. I tried to watch my step while weaving in and among the tables and crowd of dancers and minglers in the barn; there were close to a hundred people there, and it made for a bit of difficult maneuvering. My toe caught on the leg of a heavy table and my chin and palms met the dirt floor with a whump totally unbecoming of a lady. Most people didn't notice, but the boys I'd swiped the beer from sure did. Tolly and his buddies roared with laughter from the spot on the wall they'd been holding up for the past half hour. The music continued. Marcel rose from a nearby table and lifted me up by the elbow, walking me to the barn door.

"You all right?" He asked.

"I suppose … " I felt a bit cross. Not at Marcel, but at myself for my own embarrassment. I knew my face shone with multiple shades of red.

"Let's go on over to the pump and wash off those hands," he offered. Marcel led me out into the night. Despite the summer heat, outside the barn it felt like a cool breeze compared to the sweltering interior. The water pump lay at the base of a windmill. Marcel stood atop the well cover and began pumping the black handle until water gushed forth.

I don't know where they came from, but as soon as the water began pouring from that pump so, too, did the tears. They streamed down my face, but no sound came from my mouth. This kind of emotion was one I'd learned to stifle, and I was not proud of myself for succumbing to it then.

Someone opened a secondary barn door for more air inside for the dancers, and a flood of light revealed my tears.

"Come on, Marcel! Get back in here . . . it's your turn!" a man shouted from the open door. A piece of hay stuck to the side of Marcel's shirt. I nearly reached out and brushed it off him but didn't. I dropped my gaze.

"Just a minute now . . . I'll be back in a minute!" Marcel yelled back, his eyes lingered on my lowered face. "Let's wash off those hands," he said to me. Gently, Marcel's one calloused farm hand rubbed the remnants of dirt from my palms. The water felt so refreshing and cool; I longed to douse my head in it.

"Thank you . . . " I managed, although still totally humiliated.

Marcel hooked his forefinger underneath my chin and used his thumb to wipe the smudge of dirt from my chin. "There's a little more just here . . . " I looked into his eyes then and managed to keep them there while Marcel massaged the tears from my salty cheeks. He was a handsome man, with a dark, wounded expression that made me want to kiss his eyelids in defiance of all appropriateness.

"Don't you worry about that spill, now! It happens to everyone," Marcel assured me.

I'm not sure what came over me, but I had the uncontrollable urge to prove to Marcel that I wasn't just some little girl who'd tripped over a table leg. That embarrassment made me feel ridiculous and childish. Although it wasn't the best way to prove to Marcel that I wasn't just a stupid kid, it burst forth from my mouth anyway. "I didn't just trip . . . I think I'm a little drunk!" As soon as I uttered it, I felt even lower. I don't know what came over me. Maybe I thought that Marcel might consider me older than I was if he knew I could drink a few like the men and women I'd seen at these things. Drinking and dancing, laughing and

69

cavorting as if they didn't have a care in the world.

"Elsie! I'm surprised at you!" Marcel's eyes lingered on me and made me feel self-conscious and confident all at the same time, if that's possible.

A flood of laughing couples poured out of the barn and into the night, disturbing the moment. "I'd better get back. Enough beer!" Marcel pointed at me, smiled, and turned back to the barn. And there I stood. Left in his wake like an afterthought... a dumb kid.

When he left, I noticed my stockings were soaking wet down into my shoes. The pump still trickled, and I hadn't even noticed. I watched Marcel walk away and felt a horrible loneliness. It was too late to ride home with Mama and Papa; they'd gone. William and Minnie were likely not ready to go yet. I pictured Minnie beaming around the dance floor and William playing cards with the other men. I'd angered the only people my own age. I felt awful sorry for myself and decided the only way to improve my lot was to encourage Minnie and William to go. I looked and looked for Minnie, hoping that she might be getting tired and could be talked into it. She certainly wasn't in the barn. I searched around all the outbuildings thinking she might have gone away from the lights to look at the night sky. She wasn't there, either. The last place to check was the house. Although it seemed that all of the ladies were in the barn, Minnie could have gone inside to help clean up.

I creaked over the porch boards in my soaked feet and walked into the soft glow coming from Nell's kitchen. In the light, dirt stains dominated the front of my dress, and I could see that the palms of my hands were red from the quick confrontation with the ground. My anger flared up, and I grasped the porch door, bouncing it hard against the side of the house. I looked inside, and my eyes met Minnie's as she sat at the kitchen table. Her face was red and teary. The freckles spattered across her nose, and her cheeks glistened with salty wetness. Surprised, Minnie rose quickly, without acknowledging me at all. It wasn't until that moment that I realized I was just about as tall as she was. Minnie was not a tall woman, with a slight but muscular build. It surprised me that I would soon pass her height. She disappeared into the dark of the house and left me standing angry, confused, and unsure of what to do next. I knew enough not to follow her. When Minnie was in a mood, it was best just to leave her to it, Mama said. I'd never actually seen one of these "moods," but I'd heard enough about them from my other sisters who snubbed her unusual ways. Mama tolerated her and seemed to understand Minnie's eccentricities. "They always pass," Mama told me. "There's no talking to her. If she should get that way while you're staying with her, just go out for a walk or make yourself useful. When you come back, she'll be right as rain. Minnie just has more superstitions than the rest of us, is all."

Nell's kitchen chairs called out to me and I yawned, realizing that I was more than just angry, I was tired as well. I thought of my cool pillow back at home and the warm milk Mama made for me when I felt blue or had a hard time falling asleep. I slumped down in the wooden chairs and laid my head down on the table. Deep grooves and knife nicks traced haphazard lines across the surface and I followed them with my fingers until my eyes began to get heavy.

A deep, earthy scent came from baskets on Nell's table. Standing upright and proud, handfuls of green beans and purple and white dragon's tongue nodded amongst one another. Slender crimson beets beaded with moisture, just picked today and waiting for me. I loved the way that beets tasted the exact same way they smelled. There was no charlatan effort there. Beets were what they said they were.

Minnie may not have been much of a baker, but she was an ace in the garden. She grew scads of things, some of which I'd never seen before Minnie showed them to me. Mama grew some vegetables to serve to our customers at the hotel, but she bought most things from local grocers because our small yard could not hold all we needed. Minnie had space to spare and used it to her full advantage. Immense yellow and burgundy sunflowers bobbed their heads on the south side of the barn and reseeded themselves every year. Cardinals and blue jays competed for the ripened seeds. At the foot of these giants lay a fifty-by-fifty foot patch of earth upon which sprawled pumpkins and gourds, watermelon and cucumbers. Apart from this space was another equally as large where dozens of other things sprouted and ran with the rich, Iowa soil.

The garden was not work for Minnie; it was a respite. Even when there was weeding or watering to be done, she would fondly gaze upon the growing things as if she wished to take their place. "Wouldn't life be so much simpler to be a flower or a tomato plant? There would be no questioning what your purpose in life was or whether or not you were doing the right thing. Your one choice would be to *grow*."

One late summer afternoon, Minnie and I played a guessing game. She'd been trying to teach me about seeds and plants — their individual needs in order to thrive. Sun or part sun. Shade. Moist soil or dryish. Plant in the light of the full moon, or plant in the blazing heat of day. Which plants liked one another and which ones didn't get along at all. When to thin crowded seedlings and when to walk away, and let them fend for themselves.

In the early evening, we sat on the front porch. A fine westerly breeze brought relief from a day so hot one couldn't walk barefoot upon the dirt for fear of blisters. Dinner had been cold sandwiches and cucumbers from the garden; Minnie didn't heat up the kitchen much during those sweltering summer days. Cooking was mostly reserved for the winter months when the heat of the stove could thankfully help warm the house as well.

Minnie blindfolded me with one of William's handkerchiefs. The setting sun worked its way through the folds, but other than light, I couldn't see a thing.

"What am I going to do?" I asked.

"You are going to tell me what you know. Every seed has a story to tell. You see if you can tell me what story that is. Now, I'm going to place a seed in your hand. Use all of your senses to see if you can guess what it is. I'll give you some clues if you need help."

"Got it!" I smiled. Games with Minnie were always fun.

"First… an easy one," Minnie informed me.

The first small seed felt a little slimy as if it were just pulled from the fruit. It smelled sweet and was wider on one end than the other. She was right. That was an easy one. "Apple!" I beamed proudly.

"Right! Now, I have this apple in my hand. Will it be ripe yet?"

"No. The apple will still be green. It'll be ripe in the fall," I answered.

"Correct. Now for the next one… "

That seed was unusual. It felt slightly pokey on one end and seemed to have a fairly flat top on the other. It was a little smaller than the apple seed, but I had no idea what it was. I furrowed my brow in concentration.

"You don't know?"

"I have no idea what this is." I chuckled.

"I'll give you three clues," Minnie promised. "The bees love it; you'll see them dancing among its tiny purple flowers throughout the summer, and steeped in tea it's a fine cure for melancholy…" Minnie trailed off for a moment.

I knew then what it was. That was the one medicinal plant that Mama always had around. It reseeded itself every year almost like a weed but was welcomed, for it helped to cure the winter doldrums. "Borage!" I realized.

"That's right. Here." Minnie placed the next seed in my palm, and I ran my finger over its wrinkly surface. It almost felt like a molar. It didn't have a smell to speak of, but I ventured a guess because it was about the same size as the peas that Mama made me help her shell in the summer. "Peas!"

"Right again! You're good at this! For the next you will get several of the same in your hand. They're very small."

She was right. I could barely tell anything was there. The tiny seeds were about the same size as the sesame seeds Mama used on the top of her Monday morning bread when a special occasion was on the way, but I had absolutely no idea what they were. I tried smelling them and tasting them but to no avail. "I don't know," I shook my head.

"Okay then … a few clues. You should never plant these near the peas, but keep them near the carrots because they will keep insects away."

I shook my head, still unsure.

"If you pick them early, you'll find the long skinny greens on the summer table. Late, and the bulbs should hang in a dry place for use throughout the year."

That was a dead giveaway. I wasn't terribly fond of onions, but didn't mind their flavor in some things. I was surprised that the seeds didn't hold the flavor of these powerful vegetables.

74

Pumpkin and peach, beans and radishes, kale and cucumbers. The game had gone on throughout the early evening hours.

In my half-dream state, I felt as if I were back on that porch again, hearing Minnie's laugh during our game. I rubbed my eyes and yawned. More awake than before, I realized it was not laughing I heard now; it was crying. I knew it was Minnie. There was no one else in the house.

The porch door banged open. William emerged from the dark night and brushed a moth aside as it attempted to enter the house too. I looked up at him, hopeful that he wanted to leave and I could retreat to the safety of William and Minnie's house, where I was used to staying.

"Where's Minnie?" William asked me.

I was much too grumpy and tired to answer, so I just pointed into the sitting room.

I couldn't hear the beginning part of the conversation. William and Minnie talked in low tones at first. Then after a minute or two I could make out some things.

"For God sakes, Minnie, snap out of it!" William's voice filled with exasperation.

"I can't just snap out of it, William! It doesn't work that way!"

"Then how the hell does it work, because I sure haven't figured it out, have you?"

"No…" Minnie admitted.

"What is it *this* time?"

"If I buckle it this way, I won't have another child… if I do it this way, I won't either. What do I do? I can't think of another way!"

"What does that have to do with a child, Minnie? Nothing! Nothing!"

"I know it shouldn't. But it does somehow! It's a sign!" Minnie proclaimed.

"The only signs I'm seeing are the ones that tell me it's time to get out of here before someone sees you like this. You already have a reputation, for God's sake. Let's go!"

"No… no! I can't just yet. I have to figure this out!"

"Get out to the car, or I'm leaving you here!" William emerged in the doorframe and hesitated, looking back at Minnie and shaking his head. He turned back in my direction. "If you want to go, I'm going now," William said. Although I wasn't sure who he was talking to, Minnie or me.

The porch door slammed. An awkward moment of silence lingered in the air, and then William started up the car.

I pushed back my chair and perched on the edge of it. I felt uncertain. Should I stay here with Minnie? Encourage her to leave with William? Let her be and go out to the car by myself?

Minnie shuffled into the doorway — the belt in her hands. Her fingers twisted and turned the belt as if she was trying to figure out the puzzle it contained. "I just won't put it on," she said to no one in particular. "That will hold it off! I just won't put it on!" Minnie's tone took a turn for the better and she almost smiled as she looked up from the belt and at me. A surprised expression came over her as if she didn't even realize I was there.

"Well now, Elsie… I believe William is ready to go. Shall we?"

And just like that, it was over. A nagging feeling came over me just then. Something was wrong. Something more than just Minnie's unusual incident with the belt. Something more than her superstitions and the reputation those gave her. That night, I became aware of what others believed about Minnie. It stretched beyond our family and was, perhaps, worse than what my mother thought. Worse than what *I* even imagined. But it wasn't just that. Something happened that night. Something that made things take a turn for the worse, although I'd no idea what that was at the time. Nor am I exactly sure even now, but I have my suspicions.

* * * * *

A boy by the name of Walter Winkle found my sister's body hanging from the barn rafters on a wet morning in June of 1913. He's the one who alerted the sheriff by way of his mama. The sheriff's the one who called the hotel and caused my mama to drop her best glass bread pan she brought straight from Germany.

Papa didn't take the news nearly so well. He died one week later.

The call came early in the morning. Mama wasn't able to hide what happened from me; she told me right off amidst the shards of glass all over the kitchen floor. Somewhere on the drive to Elvira, the shock wore off and I became a blubbering mess. I sobbed as John held me tight to him, and Mama and Papa made the slow walk to the barn. I guess Minnie was still hanging because I heard them talking about it later that night. We stayed on at Minnie's to sit with her body and all. I wasn't supposed to be listening, but it's amazing how much you can hear with the whole cup to the door trick. Just amazing. Thank you Mr. Phinny. Papa said something wasn't right about the whole thing. He wasn't sure what, but something nagged at him. Minnie had a rough spell a while back, but seemed to be on the upswing.

My brother John's barns burned down the same night Minnie

died. He lived only about a mile from her. Strange coincidence, right? Right? Well... if you believe that, then I've got a bridge to sell you. But you'll be surprised how many adults believed it. Certain people couldn't accept that horror existed right under their nose. They shoved it under the rug and pretended that lump under there didn't really exist.

Whenever I walked in a room, conversations flipped and people put on fake smiles as if I was five and needed reassurance. Please. Even a five-year-old could have pegged that there was something fishy going on. "William... where... disappeared... " Those were the only words I could make out before the talking switched around to burial plans and remembrances.

Where was William? Where was Minnie's husband?

They don't tell you much when you're thirteen. And a suicide to boot. That was a big no-no. Shameful. All hush-hush and whispers. I actually learned more from the papers than I did from my own family during those first few days, but the papers didn't answer all my questions. I did.

So you might want to know what the papers had to say about this whole bit. Just remember that Miss Connie Thompsen (an old maid, busybody) wrote the first one, and she wasn't too bright. I'm thinking the same was true for the author of the others as well. Honestly, if there was a school out there for investigation, there sure would have been for reporters. I don't know how someone printed all of that and then didn't follow up on the burning questions. But I did have to give the reporters some credit. As long as I could sift out fact from gossip, they told me a thing or two.

~Fire Near Elvira~
Lightning Struck a Barn on the John Edens Farm. Milk House, Hay, Horse and Cattle Barns Burned — Six Fine

Horses are Cremated.

Elvira, Ia., June 21 — (Special to the Advertiser) — During the severe electrical storm last night, lightning struck a barn on the farm of John Edens, near Elvira, setting fire to the milk house, hay barn, horse barn, and cattle barn, totally destroying them.

The cattle were turned into the field and escaped, but six fine horses were burned to death. Twenty tons of hay in the barn was destroyed. A general alarm was turned in and a bucket brigade formed, but the fire had gained such a headway that it was impossible to save any of the barns.

All right. So this was the first part of the article written by Miss Connie Thompsen. She was the "Special to the *Advertiser*." Her gossip and hearsay could usually be found there.

Something the papers didn't tell you was that no one actually *saw* lightning hit the barn. This fact was brought up all quiet around Minnie's dinner table once all my brothers and sisters were gathered. They were all much older than I was, mostly all married off, but still lived either in the Elvira area, or our city, which was Clinton. No one *heard* lightning hit the barn, either. That was mighty fishy if you ask me. My sister-in-law Nell says she was listening to music, which might explain it, but if you've ever heard lightning strike anything, you'll know that it practically blasts your eardrums right out of your head. So here's the second part of Miss Thompsen's article. Normally, her topics covered who was visiting whom, the places and times of dances, and the names of recent engagements and weddings, etc. She was probably frothing at the mouth to get ahold of that story.

~Lifeless Body of Mrs. Will Seamer, Elvira Found~
Was Daughter of Mr. and Mrs. Christ Edens of Clinton — No Reason Known for the Deed.

The people of Elvira were greatly shocked this morning to learn that the lifeless body of Mrs. Will Seamer had been found hanging at her home in the Clinton County town. It is believed Mrs. Seamer committed suicide, but her relatives and friends claim they have no knowledge of any circumstances which might influence her to take such a drastic step.

A telephone message to the ADVERTISER this morning brings the information that her husband could not be found, and some alarm is felt because of this fact. It is said Mr. Seamer drove away in his auto yesterday morning. His destination was unknown, and nothing has since been heard of him.

Mrs. Seamer was about 40 years of age, and was the daughter of Mr. and Mrs. Christ Edens, of First Avenue, Clinton. The couple had been married eight years, and had no children. Their domestic relations are said to have been of the most agreeable, and both Mr. and Mrs. Seamer have been highly respected residents of Elvira.

The body was found this morning, hanging in a barn on the premises. Walter Winkle discovered the body and immediately notified the authorities. Coroner C.F. Kellogg goes to Elvira today to make an investigation, and will probably hold an inquest.

Fire last night destroyed a big barn on the farm of John Edens, brother of the deceased, near Elvira.

Well my sister wasn't 40. She was 32. A simple thing, but still, it gave me an idea of the journalistic quality we were talking about. They were married for eight years and had no children, that much was true. And the last part of Miss Busybody's article:

~Car Left in Clinton~

The sheriff and Clinton police are endeavoring to locate Mr. Seamer, whose car was left yesterday at a local garage. His absence adds an air of mystery to his wife's death.

I'll say.

These next few I found in the *Clinton Herald*. I'm not sure who wrote these, but they certainly do leave out important details.

~Elvira Woman Found Hanged~
Dead Body Discovered Dangling From Rafter in Barn Saturday Morning — No Cause Known — Mrs. William Seamer, Daughter of Mr. and Mrs. Christ Edens of Clinton, is Victim — Husband Believed to Have Gone to Scene of Fire
When the little son of Herman Winkle of Elvira, entered the barn of the home of Mr. and Mrs. William Seamer, wealthy residents of Elvira, early Saturday morning he was horrified to see the dead body of Mrs. Seamer, aged about 35 years, hanging from a rafter of the barn. The hanged corpse was already cold. Mr. Burkell and Dr. Kaack, residing nearby, were immediately called and Dr. Kaack communicated with Dr. C.F. Kellogg of Clinton, coroner, who ordered the body cut down.

The little boy had gone to the barn to get the Seamer cow. Mr. Seamer was not at home but it is believed that he had started early in the morning for the farm of John Edens, brother of Mrs. Seamer, a mile and a quarter north of Elvira, where lightning on Friday night caused a destructive fire. No cause is known to friends for the apparent suicide of Mrs. Seamer as so far as was known she was in good health and had been preparing to attend a picnic on Sunday.

Mrs. Seamer was a daughter of Mr. and Mrs. Christ Edens who operate a hotel in First Avenue, Clinton. Left to mourn her death in addition to the bereaved husband and the parents are three brothers, John and William, of farms near Elvira, and Christ at home, and seven sisters, Mrs. Joseph Wagner, Mrs. William Jensen, Mrs. John Williams, and Mrs. Ahrens, all of Clinton, Elsie of Clinton, Mrs. Otto Reyman of Elvira, and Mrs. Gus Benson of Elvira.

~Fire is Destructive~

The fire at the John Edens farm was a serious one, according to reports, lightning striking the barn which was destroyed together with a number of horses. The glare of the flames was plainly visible from Clinton.

I can see where the writer may have been misled about the whereabouts of William. After all, wouldn't it have been logical for him to have gone to the scene of my brother's fire, only a mile or so away? The rest of the town of Elvira was there, after all. It's not like they had a fire department in Elvira. Every last person who was able to stand and pass a bucket was called in for those ordeals. I imagined someone just supposed out loud that William must still be at the fire, and presto! It was in the paper. That's how those sorts of things went. Rumor and gossip become fact in a few short hours.

It only took another hour or so for someone to realize that William was indeed, not at the fire. No one saw him there at all.

We never did end up having that picnic. It was supposed to be a family affair out at John's farm. The family did gather but at Minnie's house, and instead of having a good time, they planned a burial.

~Police Make Search for Elvira Man~

That William Seamer, the well-to-do Elvira resident, whose wife's dead body was found hanging in the barn at the Seamer home Saturday morning, left his automobile at the garage of the Clinton Auto and Supply Co., shortly after 7 o'clock Friday morning, and has not been seen since, was discovered by the Clinton police Saturday. The police and Sheriff W.E. Dohgherty are making efforts to find him. It was reported that he was going to a Clinton store, but inquiry there brought the information that he had not been seen. He was not at any of his usual haunts in Clinton Friday. When he left the auto at the garage

Friday he asked that a tube be replaced by noon and the work was promised but he failed to call for the machine.

Advices from Elvira are to the effect that Mr. Seamer may have gone to Illinois Friday, as was his custom, to purchase cattle. It is known here that he had been contemplating the purchase of cattle to feed on some property near Elvira. No person other than his wife however, it is believed, knew his destination in Illinois. There is a theory that he and Mrs. Seamer may have quarreled over the picnic planned for Sunday or over his trip after cattle and that he may have left the house, Mrs. Seamer committing suicide when he failed to return on Friday night.

Mrs. Seamer, it was learned by the authorities, conversed Friday night by telephone with her sister, Miss Elsie Edens of Clinton. A young man who rooms at the Seamer house in Elvira says that he heard Mrs. Seamer going up and down the stairs at various times during the night Friday, evidencing a very restless state of mind.

Obviously William was trying to hide something if reports were true. "I'm going to the store, I'll be back by noon... " Not only that, but he wasn't seen at any of the taverns that he usually went to when he was in town. Taverns and wherever else that means. I had my guesses, but I'll keep that to myself. Just look into the seedy history of 2nd Street in Clinton, and you'll know what I mean. As for the purchase of cattle theory, that held some weight. Everyone around there knew that William made his money by buying and selling cattle.

The theory about Minnie killing herself because William didn't return like he said he would... well, that's just plain ridiculous if you ask me. That wasn't like her at all. Whoever put forth that particular story ought to get his ears boxed.

Minnie did talk to me on the phone that night. We joked about getting Mama to make her Monday morning bread one day early, so we could all have fresh bread for the picnic. Trying to get Mama to move from her routine was like trying to move the Mississippi River over a county. Minnie seemed like her usual self. She mentioned that William might not be at the picnic and seemed disappointed about that. William was gone again. Nothing new. Minnie often found herself home alone after the baby died. William's burgeoning cattle business often took him away. She made do. Minnie had plenty of interests to keep herself busy. She loved to write letters, listen to music, and entertain. She always had Marcel for company. Marcel Masters had become a good friend of William and Minnie's. He rented a few rooms in William and Minnie's house. His was sectioned off so it was private, with its own entrance, kitchen, pantry, and living quarters. It may very well be that Marcel heard Minnie going up and down the stairs on Friday night. But I'd like to know how he was sure it was she, since there's no way for him to see her stairs from his apartment. They are all the way on the other side of the house.

~William Seamer Returns To Home~
Unaware of Wife's Death Until He Arrives in Clinton Saturday Evening — Was at Davenport — Had Been on Little Trip to Davenport — Funeral of Mrs. Seamer to Be Held Tuesday Afternoon — Believed She Had Become Despondent.

William Seamer, whose wife's dead body was found hanging in the barn at the Seamer home in Elvira Saturday morning, returned to his home Saturday night from a little trip to Davenport. He was unaware of his wife's death until he arrived in Clinton late Saturday afternoon to secure his auto, which he left at the Clinton Auto & Supply Co. garage on Friday morning.

Funeral services for Mrs. Seamer are to be held at 1 o'clock Tuesday afternoon at the Lutheran church in Elvira, Rev. H. Kuhlman of Wartburg college will officiate, assisted by Rev. Mr. Whitmyer, Presbyterian pastor at Elvira, and Rev. J. S. Leamer, pastor of St. Paul's Lutheran Church of Clinton.

It is believed that Mrs. Seamer committed suicide

84

when she became despondent over the non-arrival of Mr. Seamer on Friday night. Mr. Seamer has little to say regarding whether or not he and Mrs. Seamer quarreled before his departure Friday morning. He says, however, that he invited her to go with him. That Mrs. Seamer's mind was unbalanced is the belief of relatives.

Coroner Kellogg made a visit to Elvira Saturday and made a complete investigation of the hanging of Mrs. Seamer. While he was at the house a telephone message from Low Moor said that Mr. Seamer had been seen there Saturday morning and had boarded an I & I interurban car at Rock Creek station for Davenport. The fact that Mr. Seamer left his auto at the garage of the Clinton Auto & Supply Co., Friday morning, drew money from a Clinton bank, and then was reported seen in Low Moor early Saturday morning led to the belief that he may have returned to his home in Elvira early Saturday morning, seen his wife's body hanging in the barn and becoming frightened, again departed.

It was learned by the coroner that Mrs. Seamer appeared to be as cheerful as usual on Friday night, but did not eat her supper. From the appearance of her bedroom it was evident that she did not lie in her bed. A pillow had been placed on the floor in one corner of the room, however, with a mirror near it and a basin of water at one side. Nearby was found a knife and a towel while on a chair in the corner was another knife. There was a slight scratch on Mrs. Seamer's neck and it is believed that she lay on the pillow and attempted to cut her throat but changed her mind, washed the wound and went to the barn where she hanged herself.

The hanging was accomplished in the barn, 80 feet from the house. Standing on a work bench, Mrs. Seamer had evidently thrown one end of the rope around a rafter and placed the noose about her neck, stepping from the bench and strangling to death. Mrs. Seamer, before her marriage Miss Wilhelmina Edens, daughter of Mr. and

Mrs. Christ Edens of Clinton, was born in Center Township, January 22, 1881, and had lived in Clinton County all her life.

Now, this article just plain confused me. More questions than answers. A little trip to Davenport? A little trip? What did that mean? I guess it meant none of our business. He got his car more than 24 hours after he said he would.

I'd like to know which relatives were saying that Minnie's mind was "unbalanced." Oh, who am I kidding? I suppose it was one or both of my other sisters who lived near Elvira. Neither one of them had much to do with Minnie. They thought she was "touched." When I asked Melinda once why she didn't like Minnie she said, "She's just plain different, Elsie. Can't you see that?" Well, I didn't really know what she meant by that, but I didn't care either. Minnie was my favorite sister and the only one who really gave me the time of day. She cared for me as much as Mama and in a much gentler sort of way if you know what I mean. Those of us who were close to Minnie knew that she was doing better overall though we all knew she still suffered from the miscarriage.

I suppose it was Marcel who reported that she didn't eat her supper. She grew up with our large family around the table and never cared for anything quieter. If William wasn't going to be home, she'd invite Marcel in for some company. Lord knows he would have accepted anytime.

What in the world was William doing in Low Moor catching a train if he had a car waiting for him in Clinton? That was another train or car ride away to be sure. The theory that he went home and saw her body, got scared and left, was just plain ludicrous if you ask me. Who would do that? And how was he getting around from here to there and everywhere without his car?

As far as what was in her room… I wasn't sure about that.

I didn't know what to make of that.

January 1907

My newfound freedom at the helm of our automobile has come to an abrupt halt due to all of this snow! Despite my being cooped-up in this small town, there have been a few things going on which I would like to tell you about.

William complimented me on my ability to keep the books today. I've been doing so for a while now and we haven't gone bankrupt. Ha! I'm sure it made him nervous at first, but the bank manager has talked to him and assured him that all is well, better, in fact, than when he was doing things himself. It does give me a sense of importance to be so trusted. Before William goes off to his cattle auctions, we discuss finances and develop a plan.

I suppose it's time to get some work done around here. It's never done!

February 1908

Has it really been over a year since I've written in this last? I suppose I've been too busy to write, but I can't hold this in. We've had the most terrible news. This winter has been treacherous for all of us, but most especially for the beasts. We've lost 100 head of cattle in the worst storm anyone can remember. William is beside himself with worry over the finances. He's not the only one. Every farmer in the county has suffered losses.

We had no idea the extent of the storm until it finally broke and we emerged from our home into a world unknown. Snowdrifts twelve feet high smothered the house and outbuildings. William had to climb out a second-story window just to get out of the house. Snow barricaded all downstairs doors and windows and penned us in like farm animals. Out he shimmied from the bedroom window, and jumped a short ways down to a drift that suffocated the front porch. Then he shoveled a lofty path to the front door to let me out of my prison. I was never so glad to get out of the house! Good lord, what nature can do! I wonder if some day we might have the ability to predict such weather catastrophes. Successful farmers must be prepared, but who can be ready for such a thing?

While I trudged around the house in men's pants and boots to free the windows of the smothering snow, William left on snowshoes to check on the cattle. Snow blew in from the northwest, sending the cattle sprinting away from the worst of the wind and to a location they knew well, the low pond at the edge of our property. This place was once a location for their baths and cool summer drinks, but became the end of nearly all of them. The low pond is so far sunk down, that over 100 cattle were able to fit in the bowl in an attempt to be free of the ice, wind, and finally snow, snow, snow. William concluded that most of the losses were actually not due to the wind, snow, and low temperatures, but the fact that the poor things bunched up against one another so much, that they were suffocated or trampled by their own kind. Those remaining alive were unable to move from the carnage and were gradually smothered by the snow itself as it gathered in depth and speed throughout the horrible two-day saga.

It's hard to comprehend the suffering of so many living beings. What must they have thought as the life blinked out of their hearts?

The twenty cattle remaining had a hard time plodding back to the farm. I could hardly believe my eyes when William and only a fraction of the cattle stumbled their way back. I served him a posset of milk, liquor, and spices to stave off a cold after his horrible journey. We sat around the fire but did not talk much. Visions of death danced with the fire and kept away all conversation.

Gaining Confidences

Pure Food and Drug Act

Local citizens to be advised, most especially those who deal in the sale of animal products.

United States Statutes at Large (69th Cong., Sess. I, Chp. 3915, p. 768-772)

Be it enacted by the Senate and House of Representatives of the United States of America in Congress assembled, That is shall be unlawful for Columbia any article of food or drug which is adulterated or misbranded, within the meaning of this Act; and any person who shall violate any of the provisions of this section shall be guilty of a misdemeanor, and for each offense shall, upon conviction thereof, be fined not to exceed five hundred dollars or shall be sentenced to one year's imprisonment, or both such fine and imprisonment, in the discretion of the court, and for each subsequent offense and conviction thereof shall be fined not less than one thousand dollars or sentenced to one year's imprisonment, or both such fine and imprisonment, in the discretion of the court.

All great investigators know where to look for help. One cannot do this alone. Who might be able to get you the information you need?

Sister

Mesmerized by possibilities
Truly rivaled
With my first real challenge

This mystery that happened to be my sister
Can someone, my someone, my sister
Not only contemplate death,
But carry it through?

Or, do I seek another monster?
One overcome by plan or passion
Eliminating a life
Where the rest see possibility?

Mama banged her hand on Minnie's table and pointed at each and every one of us before speaking. Then in German, for she refused to speak English when she was feeling fiery, she said, "There were things leading up to this event that we all saw! This could have been prevented!"

"Mama," Mary broke in, "We've all known Minnie was sick for quite some time, but no one, not even you, predicted that she would go to such extremes."

An awkward silence stole over the family as Mama sank back down in her chair.

Nearly everyone in the family was there minus young nieces and nephews. Nell sat on John's lap: he at the head of the table, even though my father was present; Papa felt too ill to lead that meeting. I realized John was my favorite sibling now that Minnie was gone. He was the oldest of us and protected family like a wild beast would its offspring. In America he fit in, but he had many of the old ways that made some people around here afraid of him — not family, though. We loved him to pieces, and we trusted him. Family was everything. Some people made you feel that: like Minnie and Mama, Papa and John, Nell too, even though she was not my blood sister, John trusted her and so did I. She tried to do the right thing and had a good heart. They both smelled of the smoke from their farm fire the night before and looked exhausted.

My brother, also called William, and his wife, Martha, sat at the table, too. They lived a few miles to the west of Elvira and mostly kept to themselves. This William, whose stutter made him insecure in a crowd, was slow to speak, quiet, and gangly. He and Martha had no children at all, but not for lack of trying.

My older twin sisters, Mary and Melinda, were there with their husbands, Otto and Gus, respectively. The twins didn't have much to do with Minnie whatsoever. They were all so much older than

I was; I have no idea how these bad notions about Minnie got started and no one talked to me about it. Mary couldn't possibly avoid the drama of Minnie's death, though. She was as nosy as all get-out, and Melinda wouldn't let Mary go anywhere without her. Mary and Melinda lived near Elvira with their husbands, on rented properties adjacent to one another.

All my other siblings were in the kitchen as well. The rest of us lived in Clinton, though only Christ Jr. and I were still at home. Viola, Clara, Effie, and Atta made the trip to Minnie's as well. They were all closer to me in age but still in their twenties and married. Clara held her three-year-old daughter as she was unable to find someone to watch her, and her husband couldn't be trusted with the task.

Christ Jr. looked bored, but I think it was all an act. Who wouldn't be intrigued and upset at the goings on there? He turned out all right later in life, but sure was a pain to me when we were kids.

"Something's not right about this whole thing," Papa announced. "Something's not right at all, and we need to keep looking to figure this out." He wiped his mouth with a handkerchief and gazed down at the table in thought.

"It seems pretty clear, Papa," Melinda stated. "The coroner said as such. No one wants to believe one of our own would be capable of such a thing, but facts are facts."

At that moment, William walked in. The creaky porch door announced his arrival and ended all conversation. It was early Saturday night, nearly 24 hours after her death, and there he was, standing in the kitchen, and we all just shut up. William regarded us with his hat in his hand and rubbed it between his thumbs and pointer fingers.

Nell slid off John's lap, and John stood up. He towered over William and thundered, "Where the hell have you been?"

So William finally returned home. Supposedly he was in Illinois buying cattle and knew nothing of her death. By the time he got back, Minnie was lying in the house under a sheet of white. Mama bathed her and dressed her in a high-necked dress that hid the horrible bruises.

William had been told of Minnie's death when he came to pick up his car at the garage in Clinton. Apparently the sheriff was waiting for him there to deliver the news and ask a few questions for protocol's sake. William was a well-to-do businessman and a respected person in Elvira, Clinton, and the surrounding area. Nearly everyone knew him, or at least knew of him.

He said not a word when he came into the house. The sheriff followed him in and motioned for William to go on up the steps, where he knew Minnie would be lying. William plodded up the steps by himself. Mama and Papa shooed Christ and me out the door, so I wasn't able to hear the sheriff's answer to John's question, but whatever it was, it must have satisfied them, so that was the end of it.

Christ lounged underneath a shade tree, and I spied Walter Winkle lingering out by the barn. I already told you that my sister's body was found by Walter. He was a dinky nine-year-old who lived in Elvira. I didn't know a lot about Walter at the time, but I did know he was crazy about animals. That dog of his shadowed him like flies on cow patties. He doted on all the animals at my sister's place extra good, or well, I should say. Phinny said if you want to get anything out of a person, first thing you have to do is show a little interest in what they like. Ask them questions and such.

I decided that Walter might know a thing or two that he wasn't telling the sheriff, so I walked outside and approached him. Looking up, I noticed the dark clouds moving in on us again. That must have been the wettest June on record. The last thing we needed was more rain. My shoes and the hem of my dress were splattered with mud.

I could see him near the pig pen, chewing on grass and slopping the hogs while his dog played about at his heels, chasing a goose halfheartedly.

I sidled up to him all natural and said, "You're pretty good with animals, I hear."

"I guess so," Walter replied.

"That's awful good of you to keep on doing your job after what you saw the other day." I thought compliments were in order and might break the ice a bit.

"Maybe. Someone's gotta do it."

"You go into the barn since...?"

"Had to. Someone had to take care of the cow. Milkin' and such. That's my job, and it's not like Mr. Seamer was around the last few days was he?"

I asked, "What do you know about that?"

There was a long, uncomfortable silence where neither of us knew what to say.

"I like it here," Walter said quietly. "It's quiet. Not like my house. Mrs. Seamer and I talked about stuff sometimes. I guess we won't be doing that anymore."

"What did you talk about?"

"Music... and well... I come here even when I'm not working 'cause Mrs. Seamer had the Victrola, and we don't have any music at all at my house. I sit underneath their willow tree at night;

they don't know. I like to keep it quiet, like my own private thing. If there's still a little light from the setting sun, I sketch or make sculptures out of the willow fronds and give them to my sisters. Sometimes a friend comes with; Eddie Kaszinski likes to listen to the music too. We sit and dream and listen to Lillian Russell's voice turning round and round on the '78."

Walter hummed a few lines from a song I knew my sister loved the best because it came from Lillian Russell, a famous singer from our very own Clinton, Iowa.

When from out de shades ob night
Come de star a shinin' bright,
I spy de one I do love,
I recognize ma true love
Amid the tiny orbs ob light

Walter continued, "The words drip down the wisps on that willow and it feels like magic. I even fall asleep there sometimes."

When he paused I asked, "When is the last time you saw Minnie … before she died?"

Walter put down the slop bucket with a clank and rested his arms over the fence. His dog came up to us and wagged his tail looking from Walter to me for a pet. I knelt down and scratched his ears for a minute until he flopped over for a belly rub. "What's his name?"

"Max," replied Walter. He knelt down too and said, "I saw her the night she died. It was raining hard and Eddie stayed home, smartly enough. Max and I were perched under that willow tree again when the rain and lightning scared him home. I just moved to the front porch. I don't usually do that because I feel like it's an invasion of privacy and all, but Mrs. Seamer's records were spinning, and I couldn't tear myself away. It was either move to the porch or go home, so I huddled under the window and tried to hear the music. From the corner of my eye I spied a man through the window and looked again. I knew that William was gone; he left that morning after he and Minnie had a fight. I couldn't hear what they were fighting about, but he was yelling and she was crying, that's for sure."

Now the papers had mentioned the theory of a fight. I wondered if Walter was the source of this information or if someone else leaked this tidbit to the press. That question went unanswered though. Walter seemed reluctant to talk at first, but then he was on a roll.

"What else did you see?" I asked.

"Well, Minnie and Marcel seemed to be coming from the kitchen. They sat on the couch, and it looked like Marcel was consoling her, patting her arm and such. He hugged her to him. They talked back and forth for a while, and I rested my back up against the house again to concentrate on the music. That was when Mr. Seamer came home."

"What?"

"Mr. Seamer... came home."

"Why didn't you tell anyone else that?" I asked, shocked. I wanted to shake him! That was something! That was important stuff. What would William have done if he saw Marcel and Minnie together on the couch? I'm sure it was innocent, but would William have thought so?

"Well, I can't be absolutely sure it was Mr. Seamer. It looked like him, but he had a horse and cart, not his car. I knew that he took it in the morning to get worked on. I thought maybe the garage didn't get done with it or something. It was raining hard, and I was afraid he would see me on the porch and get angry, so I jumped off the side of the porch and went back home. I really didn't get a good look."

"Okay . . . " I shook my head. I didn't know what to do with that information. He wasn't sure it was William. On the other hand, someone came to Minnie's house that night. Could it have been someone alerting Minnie of the fire at our brother's house? The timing of these two events was fuzzy for me. Minnie's death and my brother's farm fire happened right around the same time. I decided the best thing to do was to hang onto Walter's information myself for a little while. I thought I'd try to find out some proof before I made myself look like a fool for accusing William with no assurance at all. "What time did you find her in the morning?"

"I was a little late getting here that morning. I . . . I kept waiting for the rain to let up. Finally, Mama told me to just go or Mr. Seamer might get cross with me. I usually milk the cow at five in the morning, and it was getting on to be sixish. I heard the poor cow lowing in pain as soon as I reached the house. Her udders would be full to bursting I thought. I also worried that Mr. Seamer would not be so happy with me, so I ran to the barn as fast as I could go and fell a few times cause the mud was so thick.

"When I saw her hanging there I couldn't believe my eyes. I saw her just the night before . . . You know, I stared at her and it didn't really hit me what I was seeing until Max started barking at her. Then I knew he saw her, too; it was real. I walked right up to her and pushed her foot just to make sure. She was cold . . . really cold."

"Show me. Show me where she was!" I demanded. I almost couldn't believe what I was saying, but something in me needed to know. I didn't think I could make myself go in, but I wanted to look inside at least.

"Come on. I'll show you the way."

When we came around to the north end of the main barn, Walter pointed me toward the wagon entrance and said, "Part of the rope's still hanging there. You'll see... I gotta get home."

"Walter... " I said.

"Yeah?"

"Let's not say anything about William coming home Friday night, okay? Since we don't know for sure?"

Walter nodded. "That's why I didn't tell anyone except you. I'm not sure, so it's nobody's business, I figure."

Walter left me then and there. End of questions. But I supposed I had all I needed to hear from him for the time being.

I hesitated to be sure. It's not often you come to the scene of someone's death. Let alone that someone being your own sister.

Walking up to the entrance I heard a shuffling about inside. Peering in I saw Papa moving about the barn turning over feed sacks and lifting hay bales. I stayed out of sight which wasn't hard. Papa had a one-track mind and wasn't paying me any attention whatsoever.

Each time he lifted something he convulsed with coughs and fits. Papa had been ill for a good week by that time, and it didn't seem to be getting any better. The dampness that settled over us didn't help much. He shuffled over to the workbench that Minnie supposedly stood on to hang herself and slumped over on top of it. I watched his shoulders convulse with silent sobs.

The frayed rope my sister had been hanging from swayed in the breeze. I couldn't make myself step inside.

February 1908

I'm not sure I should even be writing this down. If my diary gets into someone else's hands they will see that William has been up to no good, at least as far as the law is concerned. Surely no one can get ill from the meat? I wouldn't think so. It has been unreasonably cold here. The windows show ice crystals so thick there is no seeing outside on the north or west side of the house. Surely the meat will be fine.

After the big storm, we had farmers in and out of here for days on end. As head of the association, William had to be the one to organize and carry out the plan to protect those who had lost their livelihood. The new food and drug act prohibits the sale of any meat originating from an animal not slaughtered for food purposes. That means, animals dying from disease cannot be sold (which is a good thing)! That also means that all the cattle that died in the blizzard cannot be sold for meat, either. With no insurance protections, how can the farmer survive?

It was decided by the association members that they would not let the government put them out of their farms for no good reason. They would slaughter and sell the meat from our farm. The government need not know. It would be done just as it was a short time ago before the act was passed. William says, "As it is with most laws, there are always exceptions to the rule, and this is one exception I believe in." I don't know what will happen if William is found out. I am terrified that he and all the others will go to jail.

Farmers brought in load after load of carcasses dragged behind sleighs or hauled in wagons once the roads were cleared enough for passing. Slaughter took place in our cattle shed, and the meat was stored in the north side of the barn, surrounded by blocks of ice taken out of Brophy Creek. That was a sight; dozens of men from the community gathered at the creek with axes and teams of horses to break up the thick ice and drag it to the barn. Most likely the meat would have stayed cold enough as it was, but no one was willing to risk it.

A local black market has been established, and William oversees the sale of all meat. It is difficult bookwork — and I'm the

101

one to do it. We have more than twenty local farmers with shares of meat sitting in the barn. I'm terrified of making a mistake and cheating someone out of his hard-earned money. William says that if they are caught, he will claim that I had no knowledge of the business whatsoever. I wonder, could my conscience keep quiet if it came to that?

I don't want William to know I have these worries.

October 1910

Together, we've decided that a hired man is in order. I'm no good with the animals, and William is gone so often, we need another man around the house. William hired him. His name is Marcel Masters, the famous one-armed fighter I saw beat Red Walsh. He is rather quiet, but walks with a particular air to him that tells me he is rather comfortable with himself, which is interesting because he is missing an arm. I questioned William's choice, for honestly, how much work can a one-armed man do around a farm? But I stand corrected. Marcel is quite strong and can lift anything William can. He has found ways around his deformity. I would love to ask him how he came to be this way, but we're not quite that familiar with one another. Maybe some day.

He lives in our own house, in the separate apartment, of course. It's very nice having him on hand. He has helped me with a few household duties here and there — placing the ladder so that I can wash the windows, disposing of caught mice (I can't stand looking at the poor things!), and fixing loose floorboards, etc. Mostly he is in charge of the cattle, hogs, geese, and chickens we have here. William sometimes takes Marcel with him to feed the cattle on land he has scattered here and there.

Trust Your Instincts

Most of the time, your instincts are correct. What is your gut telling you?

Ghost

She appeared limp and ghostlike
Sleeping, sad
Dressing gown hung like a funeral shroud
A mirror of the storm overhead

A brilliant flame of lightning
Revealed another figure behind her
Cloaked like death himself
They rode together

No turning back in his mind
Each staggering step
A sure stitch in the tapestry woven here

The full moon winked
At the actors involved in this play
The director for all gathered here

Clouds a frequent and inattentive crowd
In another part of the globe
When these ingredients mixed
Unaware of all the planning

And the rain poured all around
Weeping deep into the ground
Its misery and woe

Well, my English may not be the greatest, but one thing I learned from *A Complete Graded Course in English Grammar and Composition* by B. Y. Conklin was the importance of synthesis. Take the following lesson from page 133, for example:

Combine into a simple sentence containing one subject, one verb, and phrases properly arranged and punctuated:

The old clock stopped.
It stopped suddenly.
It was in the kitchen.
It stopped early in the morning.
It stopped without any cause of complaint.

Now if you think about it for a while, you'll see that the best way is the shortest path. You can get done in one sentence what the above does in five. *Synthesize.* Figure out how it all fits together.

One. Simple. Sentence.

After I saw my Papa in the barn, I turned and high-tailed it back to the house. The rest of the family talked about funeral arrangements. They planned burial for Tuesday. Mama wanted "Amazing Grace" to be sung while Minnie's coffin was lowered into the earth forever. For some things, they needed William's opinion.

Mama asked me to knock on the door and see if William might come down to talk over finalizing things with the pastor. John, Nell, Mary, and Melinda were still there to help with the arrangements as well, and they needed to get back to their families.

I took the groaning stairs one at a time while I considered my approach. I knocked slowly four times thinking that four showed that I was serious enough to stay and wait but respectful enough not to sound too eager. I had to play my cards right. I couldn't let William know I suspected him.

Ten seconds later I heard William walk across the hardwood floor and turn the doorknob. He looked down at me with a solemn expression. I was shocked at the look on his face, to tell you the truth. I was fairly sure of his guilt at that point and expected him to be faking tears or dabbing his handkerchief at nonexistent ones.

"Mama would like to speak to you. About funeral arrangements and such."

William slowly nodded his head but said nothing as he brushed past me and plodded down the steps.

Could he be innocent, I wondered? Maybe that was all just my childlike attempt to disprove the unthinkable. I couldn't contemplate suicide. I couldn't contemplate it for myself, and I couldn't contemplate it for my sister. That certainly didn't mean that it didn't happen though, did it?

William meant to shut the door. His hand lingered on the doorknob long enough to draw it closed, but he did not stay to watch my foot get in the way. I walked in and pretended that my sister's dead body wasn't really there. I had important things to do.

I'd already paid my respects. Mama and I spent a few moments with Minnie just a few short hours before. Mama sat on the edge of the bed and gazed at her. She held Minnie's hand and did not speak a word until I said, "Is it time to pray for her, Mama?"

Her reply was not one I expected from my mother — while I always assumed she was a devout Lutheran, we never did talk much about God. We attended the St. Paul Lutheran in Clinton but did not say grace at mealtime. We were taught appropriate bedtime prayer at church, but my mother did not lie next to me to help me with the verse. Prayer was private, but expected.

"Those in hell cannot be helped by prayer, and those in heaven have no need of our prayers," she said.

So it was that thought that hung over me then as I looked around for clues. Matter of fact — my sister was dead, and there wasn't a thing I could do for her save help to find out why she died.

Sheriff Dohgherty had already been through that room. It was unlikely that I would find something he had missed. On the other hand, those men were undoubtedly searching the room for protocol's sake alone. Everyone assumed that Minnie killed herself. What they saw in the room only confirmed their assumptions.

I heard out the stairway window as the sheriff spoke to my papa that morning, "We found some things in her room. Knives, a towel, a mirror, a pillow out of place. We think your daughter may have tried another way before resorting to..."

Papa nodded his head and held up a hand in dismissal, not able to listen to the rest.

Minnie's closet looked to be in order — dresses, shoes, handbags, a hatbox. The knives were no longer in the room as far as I could see. The towel was gone. Mama used it to bathe Minnie before dressing her and threw it in with the rest of the wash. The pillows were all arranged on the bed. The other object that the sheriff spoke of was lying on the vanity. I picked up Minnie's mirror hoping to catch the glimpse of a clue, some piece of something to lead me. Half of my mousy brown hair and freckled face stared back at me.

I saw nothing in the mirror to help. Just Minnie's body lying on the bed, all in white. I began to feel uncomfortable. You know the feeling you get when someone is looking at you? You can just tell that in a crowd full of people there is one person across the way who's fixing on you. Maybe they're trying to remember who you are, or admiring your hat. Maybe they are thinking of striking up a friendship, or ending one. This time, though, I knew no one was looking at me, for there wasn't anyone else in the room. I felt scared the way I did when coming up from the cellar by myself. I knew nothing was down there, but each time I came back up the stairs I looked over my shoulder several times and fought the urge to scramble back up. My imagination got the better of me again, and I whirled around to face the bed where Minnie lay. In my irrational fear, I let go of the hand mirror, and it slid across the wood floor, settling somewhere under her bed. Thank goodness it didn't break, for that would have been a stroke of bad luck as I've never had in this life. "Oh, Lord," I thought. "I have to get it. And there it is, somewhere under *there*."

I remembered hearing that sometimes bodies move after death. Fluids settle, or gases, or something like that. I couldn't have taken it if I was on my knees searching for the mirror, and one of Minnie's hands slid from its rested position on her chest. I imagined an arm hanging down the side of the bed to touch my braid or back like an ill omen. The little hairs on my neck stood up, and goose pimples broke out all over my arms. I made a step to run from the room, only guilt stopped me. I thought, I shouldn't be afraid of my sister — alive or dead, she would never hurt me. There it was again. My childish nature came back to haunt me. And I'd been trying so hard to be grown up.

I opened the door wide, so I could hear the family talking downstairs. Somehow, that made me feel more comfortable. I took the afghan at the foot of the bed and placed it over Minnie's arms, tucking it underneath her body to keep her hands in place just in case. I was ready to retrieve the mirror. I got down on my hands and knees and lifted the bedspread up. The mirror winked at me just under the head of the bed. I needed to lie down and scootch under a little to reach it. As I slid my hand across the floor, my fingers felt something small and round; I picked it up along with the mirror. The dust underneath the bed tickled my nose and I let out a sneeze. The back of my head struck the springs as I emerged too quickly. I scrambled back over to the vanity. After laying the mirror back down, I opened my palm to reveal a grey button, probably from a man's work shirt. Could this be a clue? I wondered. Probably not. One of William's buttons on his own bedroom floor was certainly not unusual. However, it was unlike Minnie to leave something like that lying around; she was an immaculate housekeeper. Almost too clean, if you know what I mean. Regardless, I put the button in the pocket of my dress and quietly left the room. I wanted it to be evidence.

Mama, Papa, my brother Christ, and I slept at Minnie's house that night. William invited us to stay. It was proper to maintain a vigil with the dead. My other brothers and sisters all went to their own homes. William gave an upstairs bedroom to my parents and slept on a chair downstairs. Papa coughed all night. I heard Mama get up and fix him some tea. I didn't sleep much either, but I did dream. I can't tell you about what. You might think I'm crazy. Do you believe in ghosts?

Early in the morning, the old clock in the kitchen stopped suddenly without any cause of complaint.

July 1911

It's done! A small, but monumental wonder grows inside of me after all this time. All the planned and spur of the moment stratagems to sway the workings of the world — fly catching, tea drinking, right foot forward when getting out of bed — these things and more have brought me a child. A little girl lies there, protected from harm. Deep in sleep. One breath from God. I will sit in this chair and stitch while only having good thoughts about the small, blond one running through the rows of beans and peas in my summer garden, hiding under beds while playing tricks on her father, eating cherry pie warm from the oven that drips joyously onto a spotless, white dress. My little girl.

October 1911

    All is lost. My sanity, any hope, a desire to communicate with anyone — gone. I've been locked in my room. A self-imprisonment. A punishment for the misdeed of losing my child. After being so cautious, one moment of carelessness tips the wheel and the cart is gone. Where is her soul now?

Gathering Evidence

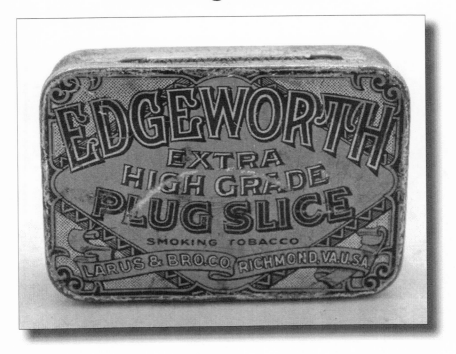

Hunt for evidence in wastebaskets, drawers, closets, books, and pockets.
Where else can you look?

"Come Down Ma' Evenin' Star"
—Lillian Russell

When from out de shades of night
Come de stars a'shinin' bright,
I spy de one I do love,
I recognize ma true love
Amid de tiny orbs of light.

Search de sky from east to west
She's de brightest and de best,
I knows she cannot love me,
Still I loves her, an' more than all the rest

Refrain

Ma evenin' star
I wonder who you are,
Set up so high like a diamond in the sky.
No matter what I do,
I can't go up to you.
So come down from dar, ma evenin' star.
Come down! Come down!
Come down from dar, my evenin' star.

Elvira didn't have much in the way of a store, but Mama sent me nonetheless to get what few things we could. She'd put herself in charge of maintaining Minnie's household.

The sharp smell of Pioneer tobacco stang my nose as I entered the flimsy door and paused in the entryway. Usually there were bells dangling from the top of a door at a place like this, but there was no sound to announce my arrival. That being said, I walked in on a conversation that I surely wasn't meant to hear. It didn't surprise me in the least — only fueled my suspicions that William was the one who killed her.

"... can't tell you how many times I heard it," said a man's voice from behind a single row of tall shelves dividing the front of the store from the back and stacked with cans of carrots, beets, and peas. My attention was drawn to the glass jars lining the counter on my right and filled with gumballs, lemon drops, molasses candy, and licorice sticks. I wondered if Mama would notice a few pennies worth of sugar bunched up in my dress pockets when I got home.

A tendril of smoke sauntered its way toward the ceiling and curled around the light fixture where it stayed like an unwavering ghost. I eased the door shut quietly. Mama was always scolding me about slamming doors. There I stood, eyeing the candy and imagining a generous storekeeper who might give me extra for being so polite.

"I'd no idea!" replied a shocked woman from behind the shelves. "I heard he was a gentleman who kept his word."

"It might be said that he did just that. He kept his word to protect his interests all right."

"Did the authorities know?" the woman asked.

"I'm sure the sheriff knew, but he and William are close friends anyway. Not much good that would have done."

"I'll be… "

"It's what happens when you have money and the right sort of friends, Molly. You get to call the shots."

"I wonder what poor Minnie thought of that. Surely she knew?" The woman inquired.

"I've no idea about that. If she knew, she didn't let on, that's for sure."

"The poor woman… it's no wonder… with a husband like that."

"The black market! Can you believe it? Right here in our little town?" With that final statement, the storekeeper's right shoe emerged from the wall of cans and I quickly pushed open the door with my heel to make it look as if I'd just walked in. I even breathed heavily to make it appear as if I'd run all the way and was now out of breath. I was getting good at this.

"What'll ya have, little lady?" he asked me from the corner of his pipe-filled mouth.

"Sugar, flour, and lard, sir," I replied.

The man was none the wiser and rummaged about the store grabbing my items from the shelves. "Now who might you be? I don't believe I've seen you around here before."

"Elsie Edens, sir."

"Elsie Edens! Are you Minnie's relation?" asked the woman who peeked around the shelves with an armload of fresh produce.

"I am."

"Are you staying at Mr. Seamer's?" she pressed.

"Yes, I am, ma'am."

The woman and the storekeeper exchanged quick glances.

"We're sorry to hear about Minnie," the storekeeper said as he rang up my items.

"Just a tragedy… " the woman mumbled while fingering bolts of fabric. "How's William?"

Both of them stopped what they were doing, looked right at me, and waited for my response.

I glanced at the floor, "I'm not sure, ma'am."

The two of them looked at one another again and the woman returned to her shopping.

In the meantime, my head tried to wrap itself around the conversation I'd just overheard. What in the world had they been talking about? Black market? The authorities? Poor Minnie? What did William get himself into? Did Minnie disapprove? And most importantly — if William was willing to break the law once, what else was he willing to do?

The man lay down his pipe in a small glass ashtray as I handed over the change.

The smoke teased my nose and reached into a memory of Minnie. This was another weekend I'd stayed with her. It was late evening. William was gone — I'd no idea where. Mama wanted me to stay with Minnie to help her out and keep her spirits up as much as possible after losing the baby. I'd lain down in the spare room upstairs a few hours before, but had a nightmare and rose for a glass of water when I heard the sound of Minnie's records playing "All That I Ask Of You Is Love," from downstairs. Lamp-light glowed from Minnie's bedroom. I peeked inside and saw her placing a small red book inside a blue-green tin. "Edgeworth Plug Slice," it said. I knew this to be a brand of tobacco. On top of the book she shoved several handkerchiefs. Then she placed the tin behind her church hatbox in the closet.

While Minnie had her back turned, I retreated to the stairs and got my glass of water. I knew at the time, that Minnie was proba-bly hiding her diary. Mama had mentioned that Minnie kept one when she lived at home. This was a source of complaint. "Always writing and never working!" Mama would say.

How could I have forgotten? Minnie kept a diary! I knew that hidden underneath handkerchiefs inside an old tobacco tin could be the solution to this mystery.

"Here you are!" The man slid the sack of items across the coun-ter and I thrust my arms out to retrieve it in such haste that my knuckles hit his pipe as it lay in the glass ashtray and set it to spinning round and round in its bowl. I hightailed it out of there and completely forgot about gumballs and licorice sticks.

It wasn't hard to find time to sneak back into Minnie's bedroom. The old tobacco tin sat behind her hatbox — in the same place I saw her put it that night. I grabbed one of the handkerchiefs Minnie used to cover the book and wrapped it up inside. What I read was far from a complete account of years. I skimmed over some. The mood to write seemed to strike Minnie sporadically at best. Minnie wrote commonly of her garden. Her acceptance of farm life. I looked for information about William and found entries that mentioned him to some extent, but nothing seemed out of the ordinary. I kept reading. I needed to find out what Minnie thought William was capable of.

* * * * *

Sometimes being thirteen had its advantages. No one suspected me of much — least of all common sense. I decided to do a little digging. I had my suspicions about William, but suspicions only got me so far. A good investigator needs hard evidence. It was time to talk to Marcel.

The back of Minnie and William's house was Marcel's entrance. Three wooden steps led up to his small porch. A red rocking chair creaked in the breeze, penned in by rungs painted white, but chipping. A work shirt and pants hung from a small clothes line strung from one end of the porch to the other, and as I knocked on Marcel's door, the pants caught in the breeze and snapped the back of my head with a light crack that jolted me out of my skin. I smoothed out my hair and knocked lightly on the door.

Moments later, I saw Marcel peek out from the curtained window to my right. Our eyes met, and the curtains fell back into place; I heard his footsteps, which were reluctant across the wood floor. The handle turned, and there he was, still peeking at me, shirtless, from the few inches of door he allowed open.

"Hello, Elsie," he sighed. "What can I do for you?"

I faltered a bit. I hadn't planned out what I was going to say, and the reality of the moment caused my cheeks to flush in embarrassment and frustration with myself. What if I was wrong? Marcel and everyone else would think I was a fool. Perhaps this was all just a child's game after all; I had no real skills or talents to speak of. Like a game of house, or cowboys and Indians, this investigation of mine was just one big act.

"Oh, Marcel!" I stumbled. "I... I know Minnie thought of you as a friend. She trusted you. I'm afraid to be staying in the same house with him."

"What? I'm a little busy right now, Elsie..." Marcel hesitated — probably waiting for me to do the polite thing and tell him I'd come back later, when he wasn't so busy. But I hesitated, too, and pretended that I didn't get it. I'd come this far. I didn't know if I'd work up the nerve to come again; it was now or never.

"Ohhh… Come on in," Marcel reluctantly agreed.

"Thank you."

"Just for a little bit, mind you. Where are your parents?" he asked, while holding the door open for me and stepping aside. His eyes swept the yard before shutting the screen door behind us.

"Mama's tending to Papa upstairs. His cough is getting much worse and now he's running a fever. John drove to fetch the doctor from Clinton. We're worried about him."

"I noticed Mr. Edens has a bad cough. It's better they've called the doc. He'll take care of him."

As I moved past him, I noticed how good he smelled, fresh and clean, and a part of me longed to grasp the muscles of his arm or feel his hand around my waist like the time we danced at Minnie's house, and she played record upon record one hot summer afternoon.

Minnie had once promised to show me how to dance in preparation for our school social. It was to be my first. She asked Marcel to come over and play the part so I could get over my shyness about boys. As we danced, Marcel gazed from my eyes to Minnie's and laughed away the hour. I felt my first pangs of attraction that day. Marcel was a handsome man. Very muscular, dark hair, olive skin, full lips. He never seemed in the least bit weak despite the fact that he was missing one arm. He carried himself with an air of confidence — like a man determined to succeed in his desires. My forgotten iced lemonade sweated all over the unprotected finish on Minnie's tea table and created a permanent ring while I gazed at him and wondered what it would be like to kiss a boy . . . or a man. Minnie played phonograph after phonograph. Marcel tried to get her to dance, but Minnie was determined to keep me in the limelight. She knew I yearned for it. As the youngest in our large family, I felt like an afterthought, a mistake. That was a good day. I started to feel grown up, like a woman instead of a girl.

"You can sit there," he encouraged as he motioned for me to sit at the kitchen table just inside the door. "I'll be right back; I'll get a shirt on."

I watched as Marcel walked into his bedroom and only partially closed the door.

"If you're thirsty, I've some water there on the counter," he called.

"I'm fine," I replied. "Thank you."

I could see that Marcel's bedroom was a mess. Clothes were strewn around, shoes thrown on the floor, dirty cups and plates poked out from underneath the bed. He sidled from one end of the room to the other, looking for a clean shirt to wear. It was a bit of a shock to see his bare chest when he let me in. I had only seen my brother Christ's, and he didn't exactly count because he wasn't a man yet. Papa was always very modest and proper. I wondered if Mama had even seen him naked.

A childlike curiosity took me over then. Although I'd no good reason to do it, I was overcome with a desire to snoop around. My right hand found a small drawer of odds and ends, but at the bottom were several photographs, unlike any I'd ever seen then or since. Scantily clad women were photographed sitting in the backs of automobiles and on the tops of pianos. The women wore only tight camisoles or men's shirts and high-heeled shoes. The back of one of the photographs said, "Love me or leave me! —Rhoda."

121

I can't quite explain what came over me at that moment, but I longed to be much older than I was. Part of me yearned for Marcel to come from the bedroom, sweep me off my feet, and kiss me long and hard as if I were as desirable as the woman in the photo. The other part of me recalled what I was doing there, and that was to investigate Minnie's death. I was certain there was something William didn't tell the sheriff and the papers. I thought, "Could Marcel know something important? Something that would lead me to an answer? He was there day in and day out. If there was something suspicious about William, Marcel would know it."

Sometimes I felt like two people. One knew common sense and consequences. I knew what was right and what wasn't. I cared about what I did and how it affected others. I wanted to root out truth and be a champion of it. The other part of me said to hell with all of that. Sometimes I wanted to just appreciate the moment as it was happening. Take a deep breath and just soak it in. Sometimes that felt like the only truth there was.

So I guess that's the part of me that took over when Marcel came from his bedroom, a blue shirt on but only partially buttoned; his chest peeked out at me. My eyes lingered on him instead of thinking about my purpose there as my fingers realized that I was still holding the pictures of half-naked women.

"I'll take those," Marcel warned me, and gently took the photos from my hand, while cocking his head to look into my downcast eyes. His one armless sleeve dangled at his side.

This sent a shiver down my spine like attraction and fear all at the same time.

"I'm... I'm sorry." I stammered, unsure what to do or say. "I was looking for a coaster for a glass. I... I guess I'm thirsty after all." It sounded silly, but it was the best I could come up with.

"Gave you a bit of a shock, eh?" he asked. "That's men for you, Elsie."

"No!" I blushed. "I'm sorry. I… " I couldn't get out the words. I ended up looking like a fool and not getting any investigating done at the same time. It was a disaster. It was time to leave… cut my losses and give up on this angle, at least for now. I turned to go. I felt like such a coward. The plan felt so right before I got there, and then I turned into a bundle of nerves.

"What brought you here, Elsie?" Marcel motioned for me to sit down at the kitchen table and took a seat himself. Sunlight streamed in at my face. I wanted to hide in a dark corner instead.

Surprised at the question, I averted my eyes and looked at the floor. There was an uncomfortable pause as I worked up the nerve to ask him.

Marcel cleared his throat. Before he could speak again, I sat and burst out with, "I just don't believe Minnie committed suicide. I think William killed her!" My own words mortified me to no end. There was no going back then. It was out. "Oh, God!" I thought, and imagined making the sign of the cross over my chest. I had to keep going now. I owed it to Minnie to follow this through, even if I ended up looking like a total idiot.

"Elsie… " he began.

"I have good reason. I've thought about this for a long time, and I think he may have killed her." Once I gave voice to my suspicions, I felt emboldened. "Mama and Papa would never believe me… I know how much Minnie cared for you. I know you were friends."

"Okay," Marcel began. "What makes you think this about Mr. Seamer?"

"Everyone knows that William spent a lot of time away from

home — not just last weekend, but often. Ever since Minnie lost the baby he's spent more and more time away. Even I could tell that. I might be thirteen, but I still have eyes and ears and common sense."

"Maybe so, but those observations alone don't point to a man's guilt."

"That's not all!" My heart pounded hard in my chest. My suspicions gained power with every beat.

"I think William may have seen something that made him angry … angry enough to kill her! I know he was wrong about what he saw, but I think you might be next!"

"Ha!" Marcel guffawed and slapped his leg. "That'll be the day! What in the world makes you think that?"

"It's Walter."

Marcel's eyes narrowed.

"Walter saw you and Minnie that night — through the window. And he saw William come home!"

"Wait a minute…" he started. "What? What did he see?"

"Walter high-tailed it home after that. He was afraid William would see him peeking in the windows."

"So why is it that you think William killed Minnie, now?" Marcel prodded.

"I think William saw something that night that made him think there was a closeness between you and Minnie. If you know what I mean."

Marcel shook his head, "William didn't come home Friday night, Elsie. Walter must be mistaken."

"I don't think so. He didn't have his car… but… "

"So Walter went home then? And he didn't come back?" Sweat beaded on Marcel's forehead.

"That's what he says," I replied. I had no reason to doubt Walter. He'd already told me more than he told the sheriff. What would he have had to hide? I noticed that Marcel looked a little panicky upon hearing my suspicions. I wondered if there was something to that idea. Could Marcel and Minnie have been… ? "No way," I corrected my thoughts. Neither of them would do such a thing. "You weren't doing anything, were you?" It was half question, half statement.

Marcel's face turned dark as he pulled his gaze from the floor to my face.

"Were you sweet on her?" I couldn't believe I was asking this, but something about Marcel's reaction made me think I was on the right track.

"Look Elsie, I don't know what you're getting at here. Minnie and I were friendly to one another because we shared a roof. She did spend a lot of time alone. So did I. She brought me pie and invited me for dinner once in a while, but that was all. Minnie and William had problems but not that kind. You need to come to terms with how she died. I know it's not easy. Poor Minnie must have been in an awful state to do such a thing, but it was done. And now we have to make do with the truth of it."

Somewhere around, "Come to terms with how she died," my eyes began to water. "Oh, Jesus and Mary," I thought. "I'm an idiot." My nose began to tingle and a big sob made its way from my heart to the space between us, filling the room. "You don't think you're in danger, then?" I bawled.

"Lord, no. Least of all from William. There was nothing between Minnie and me, so nothing to be angry for."

I shifted in my seat, unsure about what to do or say next.

"Wait," he said. Marcel slid his chair closer to mine and took my hand. "It's awful sweet of you to be concerned about me."

He kissed the back of my hand. Butterflies took over my insides and I saw something in his eyes, some darkness that showed a kind of doubt.

"I... I've got to go!" I scampered out of the house so fast Marcel didn't have time for a reply.

March 1912

William and Marcel rounded up cattle while I sat by the fire. A loaf of fresh bread cooled on the table and filled the house with its enticing smell. My hands worked over a pair of Marcel's overalls, mending the worn out places. Flurries added to the deep snow that muted the world, so that the only sound I heard was the soft pluck of the needle through reluctant fabric. I finished the overalls and reached down for the basket to put away thimble and thread when I heard another sound, something moving, something alive, right outside the sitting room window. Though we had no dog, one yipped and whined, impatient and cruel. I peered out and to my horror saw a trail of blood across the snowdrift and a small, brown leg disappear from view. Grabbing a shawl and shoving on boots, I burst out the porch door and scattered a band of wild dogs that pulled at the entrails of the poor beast. She was, no doubt, one of William's new calves, separated from its mother and desperate for life. She had survived the long trail from down by the creek, only to see death here, right outside my door. Blood seeped from belly, head, and hindquarters. Surely she could see it coming.

I did not see the men return from the field as I sat on the porch step guarding her from the dogs waiting just beyond the property line — vultures ready to swoop in as soon as I let down my guard and returned to the smell of fresh-baked bread and a warm fire.

William gathered me up and turned me around to face the door when, "Pow!" A shot rang out waking up this world, sending the dogs sprinting for Brophy Creek, and causing a fresh pool of blood to seep out over deeply packed snow. I wondered if it would ever reach the ground. Evidence of a death here.

"Not to worry, Mrs. Seamer. Animals have been killing each other since the beginning of things. One more life don't make a hill of beans of difference," Marcel advised, gun in hand. After the deed was done, he turned the instrument over to William and with his one arm, pulled the dead calf off to the barn. I couldn't help but think of my baby.

Investigating

Sometimes a detective may have to accept certain uncomfortable realities. Are you ready to discover the truth?

"To a Dead Man"
                    — Carl Sandberg

Over the dead line we have called to you
To come across with a word to us,
Some beaten whisper of what happens
Where you are over the dead line
Deaf to our calls and voiceless

The night before Minnie's funeral, Mama let me sleep on William's front porch. It was much too humid for the indoors, especially the upstairs. No one could sleep up there. William helped Papa down to the sitting room where he slept on the couch. Mama and William slept on the floor. We dragged down mattresses and old sheets for the three of us. Mine fit the space on the porch perfectly. After Mama said goodnight, I waited until I heard no more footsteps in William's part of the house, only Papa's incessant coughing. Then I snuck off the porch and peered in Marcel's windows. He paced back and forth in his kitchen, smoked cigarette after cigarette, and drank whiskey straight from a brown bottle. I wondered if he was thinking about Minnie. I wondered if he was thinking about me. After watching him for a few minutes, I went back to my makeshift bedroom.

I eased myself back onto William's porch and lay there for a while, thinking. Tucked here and there throughout the yard and underneath the house was a chorus of crickets who tried their darnedest to help me get to sleep, but to no avail. The fat June bugs slapped up against windows and clung steadfastly to screens. Those things creeped me out; I kept imagining them landing in my hair. Every once in a while I'd break out in spasms and wave my arms and legs around to frighten them away from me. When I was little I had one get so tangled in my hair, Mama had to cut it out with a scissors. Darn things.

The sounds of the insects reminded me of a summer night a few years before when I stayed the night at Minnie and William's house. Minnie and I cleaned up the supper dishes while William smoked a pipe out on the front porch. When we were done, we grabbed a quilt from the back of the couch and went outside to enjoy the starry night and the slight breeze it gave us. We walked past William and out into the large front lawn finding a clear spot uninterrupted by the trees. Minnie and I spread out the quilt and lay down to enjoy the view up above. The crickets sang all around us, and the distant sound of frogs in the creek rose and fell with the breeze. Minnie and I giggled about a boy I liked at school. His name was Marvin, which actually wasn't my favorite name, but he sure was cute.

"Have you kissed him yet?" Minnie asked.

I was nearly mortified, for I didn't think she'd ask me that, but I had to admit, "Yes… "

"You have! Elsie! You're worse than I was!"

"It wasn't so great, though. Kind of slobbery," I admitted. "I don't see what all the fuss is about. All the girls have been talking about it like it's the greatest thing."

"It takes a little practice to get it just right," Minnie advised.

"How old were you when you had your first kiss?"

"Not eleven! I was fourteen."

"That's not such a difference."

"That's what you think!" Minnie leaned over and tickled me until I squealed a plea, "I'm going to pee! Minnie… stop… I'm going to pee!"

She stopped, reluctantly.

"Don't tell Mama," I had begged.

That long-ago memory of my first kiss made me think of Marcel. I let my mind go other places. Naughty places. With varying degrees of difficulty.

Upon waking in the morning, I lashed my head around wildly, trying to remember where I was. The sun beat down on me unmercifully, the whole horrible truth swept over me, and I laid my head back down to soak it in. My sister was dead. My brother's barn burned down. My father was seriously ill. I was probably sleeping in the same house as a murderer.

The sheet Mama gave me wrapped itself around my legs like a steel trap. I'd no idea what I must have done in the night to tangle it so, but in my groggy state, it took me a full minute to untangle myself. I mumbled, "Bastard!" under my breath while I worked free of my entrapment. Sometimes I tried on new words for size, but I didn't dare do it in front of Mama. She didn't know very many English words, but she sure knew the grand-daddies. Mama was no fool. If she caught me saying so much as a "hell" I'd be holding court with a nice bar of soap.

Much too grumpy to face anyone yet, I sat on the porch steps and reacquainted myself with the sun and tried to make peace with the incessant heat. My nightgown clung to my back in un-merciful clumps. I knew I must have been a sight. Mama would fret and worry over my appearance for the funeral. I could pic-ture us quarreling over my tangled hair as she tried to brush out the knots at the kitchen table. The thought of it made me even grouchier than I already was. My sister Mary was to bring my dress for the funeral, a simple black one that I knew was at least one size too small for me. I wondered if I'd even be able to get it over my shoulders. Somehow I'd shot up just like a string bean in July this past year.

Walter finished milking the cow just then, for I heard the squeak of the bucket handle as he picked it up. Mama came out onto the porch and scolded me, "'Bout time you're up. We've only a million things to do to get this house ready for company this af-ternoon. After the funeral we'll have the whole countryside here for sandwiches, so get a move on!" Mama followed me into the house with a playful smack on my bottom to let me know she wasn't too cross with me.

I asked Mama where William was. She replied, "How should I

know? It's not my job to keep track of him!"

He was out of the house, for sure. Mama sent me upstairs to put away laundry, so it wasn't lying around for the company to see.

"For heaven sakes, don't disturb your father while you're up there! William helped him back upstairs before he left. He's running a high fever now and rambling about nonsense. He needs his rest!"

William kept his clothes in the spare room, so he and Minnie didn't have to fight for space in their bedroom closet. It was the perfect time to check his shirts over for missing buttons. As I said before, one of William's own buttons on the floor of the bedroom wasn't all that unusual. But I needed to be able to rule things out, or in, as it were. If he did have a button missing, I could easily try matching it with the one in my pocket. If it was a match, then it might point to a struggle.

William had several shirts. I clanged wooden hangers together in haste, searching quickly before Mama yelled for me or came up to see what I was doing. She would tan my backside if she knew I snooped around in William's closet. I was to deliver his socks to the bed was all. Recklessly, I knocked a shirt and hanger to the floor. When I stood back up from retrieving it, William stood in the doorway.

"Oh!" I was too surprised to cover up my reaction. What to say? What to say? "I… I… Mama asked me to put away some of your things… to get ready for company this afternoon."

William walked across the floor and approached me. He took the hanger from my hand. "I'll get that. You go on." And he motioned for me to leave with a turn of his head.

There were two shirts I didn't check. Two.

After the arrival of all my sisters, brothers, their spouses, and children, it was time for us to begin the funeral procession. Parked cars and carriages completely took over the few streets in Elvira. William and Minnie were quite well-known throughout the county. Some of them may have come out of curiosity, but most of them came out of respect. Quiet mourners poured out of their vehicles and carriages and shuffled to the church. Since it was such a short distance, our family was to walk behind the horse-drawn hearse. Two white geldings stamped their feet and swished flies away with their long tails. The driver leaned out from his perch and tipped his hat to us as we descended the stairs and lined up along the sidewalk. The undertaker motioned for my brothers to descend with the casket. They placed it gently in the back of the carriage.

I have trouble remembering many details up to the priest's words at the burial, but Papa sat in a wheelchair someone brought for him from Clinton. I'm not sure he was awake at all during the ceremony. It all seemed dreamlike. You know how that goes? When you wake, you think you might remember your dream... snippets... images. But then you move. Roll over. Feet on the floor. And just like that, you forget.

In sure and certain hope of the resurrection to eternal life through our Lord Jesus Christ, we commend to Almighty God our sister Wilhelmina Mary Seamer, and we commit her body to the ground; earth to earth; ashes to ashes, dust to dust. The Lord bless her and keep her; the Lord make his face to shine upon her and be gracious unto her and give her peace. Amen.

A slow trickle of sweat began at the base of my neck and slid down to the small of my back. It was hot, hot, hot. To add to it, I felt dull cramps in my stomach all morning. I wasn't sure of the cause... nerves, perhaps... and grief. The kind of grief that settles on you like a damp, heavy blanket. No matter how hard you try to work yourself out from that blanket, it only adds weight, and form, and more grief. During the burial, the full, ugly brunt of my sister's death washed over me and erased my childhood. I knew it fully. *My sister did not kill herself.* Up until that point, the thought was just something I played at. A fantasy. Like denial that someone is dead, except this denial was in the manner of the death. It was something to hold on to; I couldn't imagine that someone could kill herself. Especially not my sister, my second mother, my friend. Someone killed *her*. Someone *killed* her. Just then, the grass turned black, the priest turned white. A flock of grey sparrows passed from tree to tree in a frenzy. The sky... the ... My brother John held out to me a handkerchief blazing white in the sun... and I fell, awkwardly and suddenly, into his arms.

Cold wet rags. Sweat. Someone held a glass of water to my lips. Murmurs. The smell of blood. Instead of Minnie lying dead in her bed, it was me. Okay, I wasn't dead, it was only a part of me, a past, an innocence.

"You fainted, Elsie. For the Lord's sake ... as if we don't have enough on our minds today. Clean yourself up," Mama directed me, and pointed at the red stain on the back of my dress. I had felt the blood go through my bloomers as sure as anything. Minnie had told me it might be coming soon. What a strange day for it to happen. Life is anything but predictable.

* * * * *

After the funeral, both Papa and I stayed upstairs. My brothers helped Papa up, and he never came back down those stairs again. My sisters took turns tending to him, but there wasn't much to do besides keep him company. I remained upstairs out of pure mortification. I had myself convinced that my Mama or my sisters told the whole countryside why I'd fainted at the funeral. I was sure everyone saw the stain on my dress as John carried me back to William's house. There was no way I was going down there.

I spent a few lonely and dejected hours by myself listening to the muffled voices of the family and friends who gathered down-stairs for sandwiches. My mind reeled. I had too many things to think about already, and then I got my period for Christ's sake. I didn't want to be a woman yet. I didn't want my favorite sister to be dead. I didn't want my father to die. I didn't want to find out something horrible about someone my sister thought she could trust.

And then the tears came. Oh, God, they came with a vengeance. I didn't cry very much. Being the youngest and all, I was deter-mined not to act like it, usually. I had to endure endless bouts of teasing from all my siblings when I broke out into hysterics, so I taught myself to hold the sadness inside. It washed over the inside of my face and poured down into my chest where it sat and hardened, like armor. I suppose that's why I hadn't really cried for Minnie yet. Put on a brave face. Endured. I imagined myself as a brave warrior princess — valiant and strong amidst supreme sorrow. Even brave warriors break down sometime. My armor melted away.

And wouldn't you know it, at that time someone came to the door. It was Nell, John's wife. They were the ones who had the barn fire the same night Minnie died.

"Oh, honey, don't fret... " Nell walked slowly over to the bedside and sat next to me, rubbed my back. "Do you know how to take care of things?"

I looked at her in confusion, at first. I wasn't at all sure what she meant, my brain was so addled with tears.

"The bleeding ... I have some things for you here." Nell laid a package on the bed.

Lord. For a minute there I thought she was talking about Min-nie's death. "Minnie showed me how. She told me all about it," I assured her, between sobs.

"Do you have any questions, Elsie?"

I shook my head and wondered just how fast I could get her out of there. Nell meant well, but I wanted to be alone.

"I have a few more things to tell you; then I'll leave you be. We're all worried about your father. He's not well and seems to be getting worse. I think it's best if you sit with him a while. Talk to him... and... sooner rather than later. When the funeral supper is over here, we're taking you home with us. Your brother Christ will be coming again, too. We need to give your poor mother some space. She hasn't had much chance to grieve yet. She's holding it all in for you and your brother. Your father will continue to stay here. He is much too weak to move so far. The events of the day seem to have weakened him considerably. It seems his fever is back. John and I could also use some help around the farm. Our place is still a mess. The fire burned down almost all of our outbuildings. It's a miracle our house didn't catch fire." While making the sign of the cross, she continued, "Some hard work will help keep your mind off things. Another hour and we'll be leaving... okay?"

Nell rose from her spot on the bed and my body shuddered for breath the way it did when I cried long and hard.

"Oh, one last thing... Walter Winkle is asking for you."

Walter? What it the world would he want? I wondered. I shook my head. "I can't talk to him now. I'll not be coming down until everyone is gone."

Nell approached the door, then turned back to look at me, her brow furrowed.

"I'm sorry about your sister, Elsie. We all cared for her, but I know how special she was to you. I can't imagine how it must feel for you to have lost her. If there's anything I can do for you, well, you just let me know."

After Nell left the room, it was a good five minutes before I mustered up the will to go see Papa. Nell came out of his door as I opened mine and moved aside for me. We exchanged no more words, but I managed a weak smile as she moved past.

In an effort to keep the summer heat to a minimum, someone had shut the curtains and draped blankets over the top of those to keep the sun out. Papa's temporary room was so dark it took some time for my eyes to adjust. I stood for a few seconds and took in the surroundings. "Papa?"

His only answer was a horrid cough followed by an agonized wheezing. I rushed to his side and took his hand. "Oh, Papa!" My tears came back then, on the ready from before. They came with no effort at all, almost as if they had a mind of their own. I grasped his hand and laid my head down upon it.

Papa's hand blazed with fever. It was like curling up next to a small stove, and I resisted the urge to pull back from him.

"Elsie . . . " he managed to get out. Papa squeezed my hand and smiled weakly. "You mustn't . . . worry about me . . . " My father felt so weak. Only a few months before he held me on his lap like a child, and I remembered feeling overwhelmed by his strength. His old age never occurred to me, father was in his sixties yet and as strong as an ox. He was my father; he was infallible. He came to the United States with my mother when they were newlyweds — booked passage and took a chance on a new life with his bride. They moved to Iowa when promise of affordable farmland reached the slums of New York City. Papa was no farmer, but he knew that with the farmers would come all kinds of business in Iowa cities and he set out to start a hotel like that of his own parents in Berlin. Mother and Father began the Farmer's Home in Clinton. Their specialty was catering to the Iowa and Illinois farmers who crossed the river and needed a place to stay for a night or a weekend. Shortly after the establishment of the business in Clinton, Minnie was born, their first. Years later, Minnie met William right there at the hotel. She waited on him during dinner one night and that was all she wrote, I guess.

"Suicide… " Papa wheezed. "Minnie didn't do it… her feet."

Her feet? What in the world was he talking about? I wondered, but stayed quiet.

"No one else will listen… too sick… believe I'm not thinking clearly."

"What is it, Papa?" I asked.

"Her feet were… clean," he managed.

Her feet were clean? What kind of thing was that to say? Papa really was far gone, I thought. He's rambling. I shook my head and furrowed my brows in concern and confusion. Then Papa grasped my hand so hard I heard my bones crack.

"Listen… think… It was raining all afternoon. There's 75 feet — all dirt — from the house to the barn. She was barefoot. Her feet were clean when they took her down. *Clean.*"

It took a moment for Papa's information to sink in, but it did. Papa saw it all over my face. My jaw dropped and my eyes widened.

She couldn't have walked all the way from the house to the barn in the pouring rain without getting her nightgown and her feet all muddy! Someone must have carried her!

I pulled my hand from his grasp and began pacing the room. Back and forth, back and forth I went at the foot of his bed. I wasn't the only one who thought Minnie didn't kill herself. My father knew it, too. He'd just been too sick to do anything about it. It was my job to make sure this thing was seen through to the end. My job. I held the pieces. They weren't in the right places yet — just a mixed up jigsaw puzzle spilled at my feet.

I longed to share everything with him. What a relief I felt at that moment, knowing that someone else had similar suspicions! I couldn't tell my mama, though. I knew what she would do if she heard my thoughts on the matter; she'd keep me away from Papa for longer than just a day. She would be afraid that I'd upset him, and he would get worse.

Mama walked in with the doctor. The moment was gone.

"Elsie, it's time to get ready to go now," she informed me. "You can see him when you get back tomorrow."

Mother shooed me from the room with a wave of her hand. With a nod at Mama and a backward glance at my father, I ran back to my room to think.

It took time, cunning, and common sense. But eventually I did it. For Father. For Myself. For Minnie. And most of all… for revenge.

* * * * *

My brother Christ and I didn't spend much time together. Papa wanted him to learn the way of the farm in case he decided to take up the profession some day, so Christ was usually off on the farms of one of our many siblings learning this and that, while I stayed at the hotel and worked in the kitchen or served customers. My only reprieve was when Minnie would come and get me.

Since Christ and I didn't spend much time together, we didn't know one another very well. We had a bond when we were little, but that faded. Our only contact consisted of teasing and mild forms of torture.

140

Christ was particularly fond of sitting on my torso while holding down my arms and spitting long tendrils of saliva into my mouth. We were the last two in the pecking order, and he wanted to let me know who was boss over whom. The last time he did it, though, Papa walked in on it and took a belt to him. He must have threatened him within an inch of his life because Christ didn't look at me for a week after that. Served him right.

Christ and I had to share a room at John and Nell's. Their house wasn't nearly as big as William and Minnie's. We were both so tired from the recent events, that we passed out soon after our heads hit the pillow.

The fierce summer sun and relentless heat woke us up early. My body refused to sleep any longer; I could hardly breathe. Christ stood at the sole window in the room and looked down upon the fire's devastation.

"Look," Christ encouraged me. Sleep gathered at the corners of his eyes and his hair swirled over to one side of his head. "They're finally taking away the horses."

"What do you mean?" I asked.

"Six horses burned in the fire. They lay to rot in the sun for days until the insurance appraiser could come and see the damage for himself. They wouldn't give John the money until they had proof. He finally came yesterday."

The fire burned up all but the bones and blackened flesh on two of the horses. The others were more recognizable and horrific. Like something from a hellish dream, the flesh of the remaining horses hung in shreds. The bowels of one oozed from the belly and collapsed onto the dirt where maggots crawled and flies buzzed in relentless swarms. A dried pool of blood spread through the now darkened earth where someone put one of the poor beasts out of its misery.

As monstrous as the scene was, I could not turn my face away. I tried to imagine the pain and terror the poor horses must have been in as the inferno raged through the barn. The doors were shut tight, so even if they were able to break free of the ropes tethering them to their stalls, they could not break through the boards and brick penning them in. It all happened so fast, no one was able to get close enough to let them out. To be burned alive; I could not imagine the heart-bursting terror. I hoped that they did not suffer much before passing out from the smoke.

John and a man I did not recognize tied the bodies onto the back of a wagon; both men wore handkerchiefs over their noses to ward off the grisly odor. "Where are they taking them?"

"We dug a big hole along the fence line yesterday, just there," Christ pointed out. I saw the mound of earth turned up and waiting patiently in the sun. It was a good two hundred yards from the house and tucked up next to prairie grasses and red cedar.

"Breakfast is ready!" Nell called from the kitchen below. "Let's eat early so we can get outside and get some work done before noon. It's going to be sweltering today!"

Nell's voice called me away from the nightmare before my eyes, and for the first time, I noticed the cloying smell of bacon and eggs. Then I thought of the cooked horseflesh and bile rose in my throat.

"You're looking a little green there, sis," Christ teased. I managed to hold off until Christ left the room and retched into the chamber pot.

I felt like a miserable human being that morning, and then I remembered I had a job to do. The barn there at my brother John's was a place I planned to look for clues. The timing of the fire and my sister's death was not a coincidence. I believed it was carried out by the one person who didn't want anyone near Minnie's house at the time of the crime. A person who knew that everyone in town and the near countryside would show up to fight any fire together. William and Minnie's farm lay right on the edge of town with several neighbors within two hundred yards of their front door. Any foul play would have been noticed.

After feigning my way through a breakfast I could not eat, I went with Christ out into the yard to separate trash from salvage. I used a small handkerchief in one hand to cover up my nose and poked through burned wood for clues. Here are the things I found:

Raw edges of splintered boards
Tin can of snuff from Plugtown
Matchsticks of hay curled and black
Blackened axe handle and charred blade
Melted saddle and wisp of a bridle
The letters "Fe –" from a feed sack
Tin cup John used to keep stray nails
Wagon wheel rims damaged in spring ruts
Watering can burned of all possibility
Tendrils of shrunken rope
Spilled bucket of horseshoes
Metal tines of a hayfork
Three rungs from the hayloft ladder

Christ found a whiskey bottle. "Hey, Elsie, look at this!" he called, and held the amber bottle into the light of the risen sun. "J.F. Cutter, Trademark, San Francisco," it said. My brother John did not drink. Not a drop. Perhaps Nell? Unlikely. If she wanted to stash a bottle of whiskey, the kitchen would be the best place for her to keep it. John had no hired men.

Christ pretended to take a long swig of it.

A small, but persistent sound began off to the east. Flies buzzed around me, and the sun beat upon my back and head. I lowered the hand that held the handkerchief to my nose, and a thread of death found its way to my consciousness. But it was the far-off sound that took my attention, and I looked toward it. Forty or so geese in two haphazard groups approached each other. They called, cajoled, and gradually worked themselves into a single tell-tale and beautifully formed "V" that flew right over the heads of Christ and me, and pointed in the direction of Minnie's house.

May 1912

But the sun did rise today, and it brought with it a glimmer of hope that wheedled itself into my mind and shed light in dark crevices. The upturned cart was no longer there, no wheels spinning. There are possibilities now, where before there was only despair.

July 1912

William spends more and more time away from home as the months pass. Although I don't think he is with the woman all that time. I've known about his affair for several months — though I have not dared to write it down until now. There is no avoiding it anymore. Can I blame him? I've been something of a nightmare since I lost my beautiful daughter.

Wm. takes his lunch with him; he packs it himself and eats out in the fields where he is comfortable and alone. One of my lunchtime companions is Marcel, who is good company. He seems to care about my welfare. "How are you doing today, Mrs. Seamer?" And he really listens to my answers. He brings me flowers from the pastures and berries from the woods. All meant to brighten me up — and they do, and he does. My other companion of late is a boy that William hired to take care of the milk cow, Walter Winkle. The poor boy is a hard worker and bright, too, but I wonder about his situation at home. He has bruises that he explains away. Some of the excuses sound believable — fell from the hay mow... cow kicked me in the arm... got beat up by a group of boys in town... Some not so — ran into a fencepost... tripped over a rake... baby sister conked me upside the head with Mama's rolling pin. I know little of the family — they do not attend church here, but ride into Clinton for masses on Sundays. The father runs the blacksmith shop here in Elvira and the mother rarely leaves the house. I've seen her hanging laundry up outside and emptying the slop bucket, but she walks hurriedly and is swallowed up by a house filled with children. Walter is cheerful enough, and inquisitive. The boy also loves music as much as I do! When he thinks I'm not looking, he sneaks up underneath the willow tree and listens to my records. I've no doubt he will be a successful something one day, perhaps a musician. As we get to know one another, he spends more and more time with me. Walter is a bright spot in my day.

I wonder what Elsie would think of him? He's younger than she is, but they seem alike in a lot of ways. I have not invited Elsie out here for a long while. Perhaps it's time.

Shadowing

Shadowing Notes
_____

- Appear normal
- Blend in
- Use eyes and ears
- Learn how to lie
- Use props
- Assume other identities
- Use imagination and wits

You may need to follow suspects for a time to gain information.
How can you do this without being detected?

Suspect

A man
Large, muscular
Rope burns?
Scratches on his arms and face?
Missing a button
Hateful
Set in his ways
Known to the deceased
At the scene of the crime — Friday p.m.
Motive:
To silence a terrible secret?
To dominate?
To be able to choose something —
Even though it be to take another life?

"He asked what I saw that night," Walter explained the next day.

"Why would he ask me that?"

"Who are you talking about?" I asked.

"Marcel. Marcel stopped me in the barn yesterday and asked me about the night Minnie died. Why would he ask me?"

"I don't know. Maybe he's starting to think William's guilty, too."

"Maybe."

"Maybe he and Minnie really were doing something that made William angry... "

"Like what?" Walter inquired.

"Kissing... holding each other. Didn't you say that Marcel was comforting her when you looked in the window?"

"Yes."

"Well... I suppose it's possible that more happened after that."

"I suppose."

"And it's possible the other person you saw that night was William, right?" I questioned.

"It sure looked like him."

"Maybe we have an adult on our side now, Walter."

"We could use that," Walter acknowledged.

"He didn't seem to believe it was possible that William killed

Minnie when I talked to him before, but maybe he's changing his mind. If we find out more, we can always go to Marcel. I think I need to tell you what I know. Then we can talk it over together and decide what's best." So I told him everything. I flipped through my notebook and showed him some of my notes and sketches. I told him about what my father said about Minnie's clean feet. I told him about the bottle and the button. We decided to find a time when I could sneak in and finish looking for the clues I needed to prove guilt. Most importantly, whose button was it, and did William drink J.F. Cutter Whiskey?

The rest of Thursday and most of the day Friday we looked like old pals chumming around the farm. We lurked about and appeared as if we were playing a riotous game of cowboy and Indian, when really we were searching for a good time to look for the whiskey without Mama finding out. William left earlier in the day but was due back anytime. Marcel was hard at work as usual — in and out of the various outbuildings, never stopping to rest.

Mama called me in a few times to ask me to help out with this and that. Walter hung around and waited for me. I emptied Papa's chamber pot, swept the kitchen floor, and sat with Papa a few times and held his hand. I died to tell him about my thoughts regarding Minnie's death, but it wasn't the time. Papa was not well enough and I feared the stress would make him worse. "I remember what you said, Papa," I reassured him. "I remember." Papa only squeezed my hand in reply. His fever was high and he seemed to be disoriented. I saw it in the haunted look in my mother's eyes. She waited for the inevitable; Papa would die. Soon. The doctor didn't bother coming any more. Nothing could be done. She needed not speak the words to me. I could tell by the slumped posture in her shoulders. Something finally beat her down. Her hair, normally in a tight, flawless bun, came out in unruly wisps from the nape of her neck. Her dress, usually crisp and clean, hung undisciplined in the damp. Dried blood from Papa's horrid cough stained the bodice of the dress and the white apron Mama wore that was once my sister's. Minnie's death did not break her, but my father's would. One more was too much. My mother may have been harsh and slow to show affection, but she did love us.

Between Mama's demands, I was able to find time to look for the whiskey. I came down from sitting with Papa and saw Walter motioning for me to come talk to him outside. I poked my head out the door, and Walter motioned toward Mama who stood at the side of the house beating the dust from the rugs.

"Look now!" Walter whispered. "I'll throw a rock at the window when she's on her way in."

"Got it!" I said, and turned around so fast my feet slid on the waxed wooden floor. I knew where the liquor cabinet was. The hutch in the kitchen had two doors in the bottom. Minnie kept plates and bowls in one; William stored a few bottles in the other. I remembered watching him pour a small glass of amber liquid after dinner sometimes. He didn't drink often, as far as I could tell, but he did drink occasionally. Did he drink J.F. Cutter? That was the question. As I opened the cabinet door, clouds passed over the sun and sent darkness through the room. I fumbled around inside the cabinet, straining my eyes to see. My clumsy hands knocked two glasses together, causing one to tip over on its side and nearly fall out onto the floor. Thankfully, the lip of the cabinet prevented what would surely cause Mama to come running. My heart pounded a little faster while going through the remaining contents: a metal flask, a light-blue Gordon's gin bottle... and a forgotten cap with no bottle to show for it. The cap looked to be the same type as the one on the gin bottle. I wasn't sure what "gin" really was, but I could tell it wasn't the dark-colored stuff I'd seen William drink before. There was no such type of whiskey here. That in itself was a clue. The dark concoction I'd seen William drink before was gone... perhaps thrown on the floor of John and Nell's barn while he tried to distract the townsfolk from the bigger crime... the murder of my sister.

Even though this felt like a small triumph of investigation, I was at a standstill. What to do with these little clues? I needed more, but I was unsure how to get it. Back outside with Walter, I decided to refer to Phinny's booklet for some direction. A chapter I had not paid much heed to was that of "Shadowing." To tell you the truth, I was scared to follow William around. Scared of what I might find... scared of what he did... scared of what he could do. My fingers followed the words, but my mind thought of the frightening possibilities.

"What does it say?" Walter asked.

I recited, "Appear normal. Blend in. Use your eyes and ears while your body tells the lie."

"What the heck does that mean?" Walter asked.

"It means, stay alert and don't get caught."

"Oh."

"William isn't even here right now. And when he gets back... I... I'm afraid to follow him," I worried.

Walter burst out, "I know! Since William isn't here, and we aren't very good at this yet, we could shadow Marcel, for practice!"

At the mention of Marcel I felt my cheeks get hot.

"Oh cripes! You're not sweet on him, are you?" Walter asked.

"No! Of course not!" I scoffed and absentmindedly covered my cheeks. I never could mask my own embarrassment. I would need to work on that if I was to become a top investigator. "Let's go practice!"

We looked for Marcel everywhere. He wasn't in the barn, the hog house, or the cattle shed. We looked down by the back pasture and even knocked on his apartment door. There wasn't much practicing we could do if we didn't have someone to practice on.

"We could practice on your mama," Walter suggested.

"She'd shoo us off in two seconds. Mama doesn't put up with much. Besides, if she sees me she'll put me to work," I said.

The wind carried a strange metallic scent to us just then. Walter and I looked at one another and wrinkled up our noses.

Walter asked, "What's that?"

"It smells like blood, Walter…"

"It does smell like blood!"

Our imaginations got the best of us as evidenced by the saucer-like shape of Walter's eyes.

"Remember, we need to blend in!" I warned.

We did little blending in while we crept on tiptoe and looked over our shoulders. My nose led me to the opposite side of the chicken house to the yard out back. Walter and I glanced around the corner and spied a ghastly scene — one common on the farm but foreign to me. Mama got all our chicken from the local butcher, just around the corner from our hotel. When it came to us it was just… meat. Not a once living thing.

Hanging by its feet from a wooden frame was a headless chicken. Blood oozed from its neck into a metal bucket making a tinny sound as it pooled in the bottom. Marcel reached into the chicken pen and grabbed another protesting hen by its neck. A flurry of feathers and panicked cries erupted from the poor thing, but she was soon stopped from all form of outcry when Marcel swung her round and round like the end of a jump rope. Soon the hen was limp in his hand and he walked over to the stump of a tree. Dried blood stained the top and sides of the old oak. At its base sat a sharpened axe. Marcel slapped the chicken down on the trunk, took axe in hand, and deftly brought the blade down on the neck. From there, the chicken was hooked on the wooden frame next to its dead companion and left to bleed out into the same metal bucket.

Marcel looked up in our direction, but my horror did not allow me to move back in time. We were caught.

"What are you two doing? Come to see how it's done?" Marcel asked.

"Just playing!" Walter offered.

I was too sickened to respond. At that point I didn't think I would ever eat another chicken in my entire life.

"Elsie! You look sick," Marcel laughed. "How did you think it was done? It's not pretty, you know!"

"I… " I couldn't seem to say anything else.

Marcel laughed. "Go on and tell your mama the chickens are ready. She should have the water boiling by now."

I didn't need any more excuse to get away from there. I tore off toward the house.

Walter called after me, "Slow down, Elsie!"

* * * * *

About an hour later all hell broke loose.

Walter and I hunched behind the cattle shed ruminating on the possibilities of bottle and button when I first noticed the clouds. Tendrils of hair slapped my face and I looked up to see a wall of charcoal clouds advancing from the northwest.

Walter, however, was stuck on the button. "It could be from a shirt Minnie was mending for either one of them," Walter mused. "Or an extra button from her button tin. My Mama has one of them — and it rolled under the bed. You know, it might not be a clue."

"Minnie didn't do her mending in the bedroom, Walter. She always did that in the sitting room." I eyed the clouds nervously.

"But, maybe… "

"Shhh!" I got tired of Walter's ideas. I'd already thought of them all myself, anyway. But something was wrong with the world just then. The air felt different, and the birds stopped singing. The milk cow lowed and yanked the rope tethering her to the barn while the flock of geese Minnie hated so much huddled under the willow tree and scuttled this way and that. Walter's dog Max took one look at us, barked in the general direction of the oncoming storm, and tore off in the direction of home.

We sat and watched the clouds for a few more minutes until the rain came. And come it did — torrents of wind-ravaged water pelted us and tried to melt us right into the ground.

I shoved my notebook in the pocket of my dress; then Walter and I scrambled to our feet and sprinted to the house. I had visions of wily tornados — three of them at once, barreling down on us as we ran. There was only one thing that terrified me in this world, and it was a tornado. I'd heard stories of homes, swaths of trees, barns with livestock, and entire towns picked up and thrown like the bath water into the countryside. One local tale boasted of a church hymnal tossed five miles southeast of its original location.

I had a recurring tornado dream where I stood at the front door of our hotel and tried to convince passers-by to take safety from an oncoming cyclone. No one ever listened to me. They looked at me — the crazy girl in the doorway, with unconcerned faces and went about their business as if there were nothing in the world to be worried about. I watched everyone go off to die, and I couldn't tear myself away from the door thinking that maybe just one person would listen to me. I could save *one*. The tornado was so close; it began to pull papers and dishes out the doorframe around me, but all the people just kept walking about, not noticing a thing. I hated that dream.

Recipe for a tornado: During the month of June, pour into Iowa the following: incessant heat, humidity, clouds from the north, clouds from the south, and a whole lot of chaos. Stir vigorously until the precipitation begins to dip to the ground. Now take cover.

We reached the safety of the house, huddled inside the kitchen door, and watched the storm unfold. A strong nor'wester hurled down upon us. The power of the wind waxed and waned every ten seconds causing the sound of the deluge to go from a roar to a raging steam engine and back to a roar again.

I watched Marcel as he sprinted from the barn to William's front door. There was only one cellar for the house, so Marcel had to take cover with us. He held on to his hat and sloshed water and mud all over the back of his pants. The area from the house to the barn was already a mud hole after only moments of rain. The clouds just wouldn't let us alone. Marcel shook the rain off his clothes and removed his boots just inside the porch. He brushed my shoulder when he walked past.

"Where's William?" Mama asked. I shook my head. Walter and I had watched him leave riding the gelding north of town. "Well, go about the house up and down and make sure no windows are open." As Walter and I went about the task I heard Mama cry out,

"Here's William!"

He slipped over the mud road as fast as the poor horse could go. It bucked and snorted in protest and seemed fit to tear the reins right from William's hands.

"Get some towels!" Mama ordered. And that was when the hail started pelting the north and west sides of the house. Walter and I stood dumbfounded, not quite understanding what was happening at first.

I watched Mama's eyes go wide, but she didn't share the thought. "Hurry now, off for the towels… it's only hail. Just… stay away from the windows!" Back in the pantry I yanked three old towels from the shelf and stopped, mesmerized by the sight out the window — ice rocks the size of hen's eggs plummeted, nesting snugly in the mud. I'd never seen such a thing before, only heard of it. I thought one of those in the right place could kill a man.

After reaching the yard, William jumped off the horse and let it go — there was no tethering the poor thing now. It was wild with fear.

Mama held the door for William as he ran in. I handed him the towels, and he regarded me with a slight nod. The ice continued coming down hard against the house. Each time one hit a window I winced, expecting to hear the crash of glass any minute. William dried off as best he could with the towels and proceeded up the stairs to change clothes.

"Come on now, away from the windows you two, " Mama directed. "We should probably… "

William paused on the creaky steps and tilted his head to the side, listening intently.

"What is it?" I asked.

"Shhh!" William warned.

All sound stopped. Just like that — the hail, the rain, the wind — all of it was over.

Mama uttered a German phrase I'm sure would get me multiple courses of soap. "Come on. We need to get Papa downstairs!" Mama brushed past William and ran as fast as her fat little legs could carry her. "You two get down in the fruit cellar and wait for us. Marcel, make sure they stay there!"

I stood for a moment, not understanding what was happening. Then Walter uttered, "Tornados follow hail, Elsie. We'd better go!" A short flight of stairs led from the pantry down into a small room where Minnie stocked potatoes and canned goods. It was also possible to enter the cellar from a rickety door outside that pulled up instead of out. Walter grasped my hand and started for the northwest kitchen window.

"Jesus, Mary, and Joseph . . . look at it," he mumbled. We stood transfixed. It was hard to believe that such a thing was true. How they are created is completely beyond me, but it seems that God's own hand stirs the pot. The mighty beast loomed on the horizon, like a giant overlooking its prey. The storm turned what would normally be a hot, sunny, late afternoon into a thing of terror. Clouds churned above us and some curled down toward the tornado so that the whole thing looked like a giant question mark every time it whipped around. Plumes of greying debris swirled about its base. It headed straight for us.

I couldn't go into the cellar before I knew my parents were okay, too. I turned from the window and took a step toward the up-stairs.

"What are you doing? Get back here!" Walter screamed.

"Get!" Marcel pushed me back toward the cellar. "Now, Elsie!"

Looking over my shoulder, I saw that Mama and William were already on their way down. William carried my father as easily as my father once carried me, only draped across his outstretched arms. Papa weakly held one arm around William's neck as they awkwardly worked their way down each flight of steps.

"Get down there!" Mama scolded.

Walter and I scrambled down the stairs, followed by Marcel. William placed Papa on the floor with his head on some old gunnysacks, and Mama shut the door to the cellar, blocking out all light and sound. Then a roar began over our heads and chased away the silence. Walter and I held hands in the dark.

"I hope Max got home," Walter worried.

"Don't you worry about that dog," William said. Animals know better than we do when it comes to these things. He'll be all right." A match was struck just then and William lit the lantern. Not trusting it to be hung on the peg, he clenched it in his fist.

The lantern swayed slightly, causing dancing shadows and light to streak across our faces. I broke from Walter's grip and Mama and I huddled on the floor while each of us took one of Papa's hands. He coughed weakly and squeezed mine. William, Walter, and Marcel took seats on the barrels and boxes they could find.

No one said a word. I looked up and saw Minnie's canned goods that lined the shelves near the outside door. Strawberry jam, carrots, beans, peaches, apple pie filling, corn. Funny that such small things can survive a human life. It didn't seem right that those items that existed because of my sister didn't just disappear after she was gone. I thought, How dare they survive her? Mama followed my gaze and read part of my mind, no doubt. She reached over to me and squeezed my arm — a small gesture of understanding.

Outdoor sounds were muffled, but we could still hear the chaos. My ears popped and a high-pitched whistling sound worked its way into the house and snuck into the cellar where it taunted and teased us with its malevolence. I twisted around in a vain attempt to locate the source of the sound, knowing very well that the source was beyond my sight. William sat with his head in his hands. Walter hugged his knees and stared at the ground. Mama shut her eyes and prayed. Papa was half-asleep, but coughed again, splattering more blood onto his nightshirt.

The house creaked and groaned. Glass crashed to the floor upstairs. I pressed my hands over my ears to block out all noise, causing the cacophony to sound like a million bumblebees surrounding the house. I expected the lot of us to rise up any second and get tossed into the next county.

My tornado terror reached its peak when the door leading to the outside flung open violently and leapt from its hinges. I screamed and hunched as close to the wall as possible. My hair and dress strained to join the chaos outside. If that tornado wanted to take us, nothing we could do would stop it. We all knew that. Jars sprung from the shelf and out into the storm. Some hit the sides of the doorframe and came crashing back onto the stairs and at our feet, splattering an unruly mix of red, green, and orange. A gunnysack that had been draped over the railing lifted up into the air like a butterfly, held itself in the air for a moment, and disappeared out the door.

To tell the truth, I don't pray much, but I did then. I prayed that the farm would be intact. I prayed that my father would somehow live. I prayed that Minnie's killer, who sat right in that room with me, would die a horrible death. I prayed I'd get to watch it. Little did I know, that was all the calm before the storm.

December 1912

I wish the world could always be as it is now. A light snow fell this afternoon, followed by a gale of white, fierce and intent upon bending our world to its will. Like mother's warm blanket around unwilling then grateful shoulders. These moments are pure and magical, untainted and naïve of all evil. If there is such a thing. The snow covered it all up, hiding it from view and from our conception of reality for a time. And then someone takes a step, or tire tracks mar a perfect entrance. But not yet. Not now. Now the blanket is pure and unbroken. No mud, no tracks of rat feet or sparrow. No need for better days, better hours, better attitudes... All is right with the world.

Inspecting Places

If there is a crime involved, the scene of the crime must be explored. What can you find there?

Clues

Sometimes
One
Can
Find
Clues
In
The
Least
Likely
Of
Places.
Look
Anywhere
And
Everywhere.
Look
At
Everyone
And
Everything.
Keep
Your
Eyes
Peeled
And
Your
Mind
Open
To
Even
The
Most
Horrific
Possibilities.

It's hard to talk about what happened after the tornado that day. I can't tell you just now. I have to warm up to telling it. I feel ashamed a bit, I suppose. For not seeing earlier, what was there the whole entire time. That signals like church bells did not blast me from my seat and knock me flat. The signs came much too late.

As we sat in the cellar, sounds from outside gradually stopped altogether and dominant then were the noises of a chorus of breaths. Me rabbit-like and unsure, Walter a bird in the new-fallen snow. Papa halted and spare, Mama defeated for now. Marcel even and patient, William an animal dormant in the haze.

We huddled like that, breathy and quiet, for several minutes before William spoke. "Sounds like it's over. You all go on out. Walter, you'd best head on home. Marcel, you take Mr. Edens back on up to his room. I'll clean up this mess here." He motioned to the scattered pile of smashed glass, battered fruits, and wasted vegetables that the tornado tried to steal from the depths of the cellar. Only a few jars remained untouched. One jar of peaches perched precariously on the edge of its shelf. William grabbed the broom and swept the bulk of the mess down off the stairs and to the side so we could get out.

"Go on now," William encouraged Walter and me. "And Marcel, when you're done, head on out to check over the house and buildings for damage.

Marcel nodded at William, and with Mother's help he leaned over to lift up my father.

Walter and I led the group out into the yard. Mama followed us; then Marcel carried my father. The tinkling sound of broken glass came from the cellar as William swept up the damage done there.

The five of us stopped to survey the chaos. Three old pine trees in the yard appeared disheveled, with several branches half burst off and dangling, precarious, just to our left. Shingles from the house and outbuildings lay haphazardly across the entire farm. A few wooden slats from the side of the house reached out from the frame and pointed at the barn where the most noticeable damage was the roof itself. One half of the barn roof appeared to have been sucked right from the top. The wooden framework thrust up into the sky like begging fingers. Hay from the mow dusted the ground and collected in foot-deep drifts. The only animals we saw or heard were a few brave and battered birds tentatively chirping and yet to come from their nests. The geese and farm cats were nowhere in sight.

We slowly picked our way through the rubble around the house and saw that numerous windows were broken and tree limbs were down everywhere. One had burst through a window in Marcel's apartment.

"Looks like I'll be cleaning up more glass in the house," Mama realized. "Let's get you settled," she said to Papa, "then I have some work to do." Mama took his hand and rubbed it briefly, then broke the gesture and led the way into the house. Marcel followed.

"I'll be damned," Marcel muttered while gazing at the devastation. "I'd better get you on up, Mr. Edens."

Things were so quiet. It was hard to reconcile that new calm with the pandemonium the tornado brought through there just a few short minutes earlier. Even the clamor of William sweeping up the broken glass in the cellar faded completely.

"Max!" Walter cried out, breaking the peace. He called for him several times and from the direction of Walter's house, Max came running, anxious and excited to see him, but his tail was between his legs. Walter kneeled and buried his face in Max's fur for a little while. "Good ol' Max. Good boy." Then Max sidled by me in greeting, and I gave him a pat.

Walter and I walked over and sat on the white painted fence connecting the barn to the pasture when I felt around for my notebook. I usually kept it in my dress, and it wasn't there. I thought maybe I left it in my bedroom upstairs but remembered going over my notes with Walter just before the storm. "Oh, no! Where's my notebook?" I began to panic. "Did I leave it in the house when we were busy shutting windows?" I didn't think so. "What if I left it lying around outside during the storm? It could be anywhere!"

"I'll go look at the spot we were in before the storm," Walter said. It was unlikely that the tornado would have left anything so light in its original place, but Walter seemed eager to help, so I wasn't going to tell him not to bother. He ran off in the direction of the chicken house. I sprinted inside and quickly checked the rooms I'd been in before we went down into the cellar. No notebook. I ran back outside and met Walter at the fence. "Sorry, Elsie. It wasn't there," Walter admitted.

I paced a short distance back and forth. Where could it be? My mind went in several directions simultaneously. What if Mama found it? She'd lash my backside until next week for all the snooping I'd done. What if William found it? His whereabouts during those two days didn't look good; he was my suspect. He certainly had motive. Lord knows what he was capable of. I had to find my notebook first. I had to!

Then I remembered. "I know, it was in my pocket! As soon as we saw the storm coming, I shoved it in and ran for the house. It must have fallen out," I said.

"In the cellar?" Walter realized. "Mr. Seamer's down there!"

Walter and I tore off like two rabbits chased by a fox. We passed the windmill, which was normally creaky and spooky but silent now, and Minnie's garden — now more weeds than vegetables. We'd a hundred yards to go before we reached the opposite side of the house where the cellar door had been torn off. No sound came from down there.

"Mr. Seamer?" Walter called.

"Yep. Just finished up down here." William walked up the short flight of steps and brushed past Walter and me. He took a long look about the farm, shook his head, and went on around to the front porch door. As soon as we heard the door bang shut, Walter and I hastened our way down. Our feet crunched over broken glass when we stepped down onto the cellar floor. William did not do a thorough job of cleaning, but Mama says men never do.

My eyes swept the floor where I'd been sitting and found nothing.

"Maybe it's over here." Walter brightened, as he moved to search between the barrels and boxes. His foot slipped on a glob of apple pie in a jar and he fell onto his rump.

"Ow," Walter whimpered.

"What is it?"

"I cut myself," Walter replied as he held up his hand to show me the small shard of broken glass sticking out from the palm of his hand. He plucked it out, and a stream of blood began oozing down onto his arm.

"I'll go get something," I promised, and I hurried into the house for a bandage.

Marcel came from the house just then, and we passed one another in the doorway. He held it open for me but no words were exchanged as I was on a mission. I didn't want to take time to ask Mama or William where to find bandages, so I ran up to my room and rifled through my bag for a handkerchief. On the way back down, I noticed that William's door was shut. Mama swept up glass from somewhere on the first floor.

Back down in the cellar, I quickly wrapped Walter's cut with my handkerchief.

"The notebook's not down here," Walter assured me.

"I know… this is horrible!" I pressed my hands into my forehead and wanted to burst into tears, but I had to hold myself together. This was serious. What if Minnie's killer was reading my notes right now? What would he do to me? What would he do to Walter? Think, think, think! I told myself.

Walter squeezed the palm of his cut hand and peered at me with hopeful eyes. The poor kid was only nine for Christ's sake, and here I'd gotten him involved with a murder. If something happened to Walter, I'd never forgive myself.

"You need to go home," I encouraged him. "Your parents must be frantic."

"I'm not going. I'm not leaving you. At least not until we find your book."

"You need to get out of here! I'll not have you getting hurt because of me." I tried to seem angry, but part of me was relieved.

"Listen, Elsie. Things aren't so great for me back home. Why do you think I'm here all the time?"

"I… I don't know. But things have to be better at home than they might get here. If Minnie's killer has the notebook, I'm dead! And you're with me, so what do you think that means?"

"I'm staying. You can't make me go," Walter assured me. "I'm staying."

Walter might have been only nine, but having him around gave me confidence I wouldn't have had otherwise. It was like clutching a doll to you during a lightning storm. You know there's not a darn thing that doll's going to be able to do to protect you, but somehow, you feel better.

"Fine. Let's go look around the yard some more. Maybe the notebook got picked up by the storm and thrown somewhere. Maybe we don't have to worry about that, at least," I said.

Walter and I inspected every last inch of the yard and adjoining pasture to no avail. Either I left it in the cellar and William picked it up, Marcel found it while inspecting the buildings, or the notebook was blown to kingdom come by the storm.

"What are you two looking for?" Marcel called from the side of the house. He'd apparently finished the inspections William sent him on and was heading inside his own apartment.

Walter and I dealt each other quick side glances, but it was Walter who replied, "Oh, we're just looking for interesting things the storm whipped up. I found bird eggs," Walter lied. "One was still whole!"

"Be careful, now," Marcel warned. "There's lots of broken glass around."

"We will," I called back.

Marcel turned around and went on inside his place.

"What now?" Walter asked.

"I don't know," I shook my head. "We can't go inside. William and

Mama are in there and could hear us."

"Let's go on in the barn. We can have some privacy there," Walter decided.

I shook my head.

"Why?"

"I haven't been in since... "

"Oh, well, maybe it's time, Elsie. Maybe you'll find a clue in there."

I couldn't argue with Walter's logic. If I was going to be a true investigator, I'd certainly need to check out the scene of the crime. Phinny would do it. It was time to go in.

Walter took a step toward the barn and held out his hand. "Come on," he coaxed. "I'll be with you."

To ease me into it, Walter said we should check on the milk cow first. She was housed in the side door of the barn, in an area separate from the scene of the hanging. The poor thing huddled as best as her large frame allowed — pressed up against the wall. "I'll bet she won't produce milk for a few days... poor girl," Walter worried. He climbed over into her stall and moved to stroke her head, but the cow jerked back, moving as far away from Walter as possible. "It's best we leave her alone," Walter decided, and he led me into the center of the barn. For a second, my attention went immediately to the dangling remains of the rope still hanging from the rafter.

"Oh, man!" Walter cried. "Look at this!" He ran over to the cause of his excitement. Max ran with him. It was the top of the windmill. The wheel and bent vane of the mechanism apparently sprang from the frame and rolled into the barn during the maelstrom. I looked out at the original location of the windmill and noticed that both the frame and pump seemed to be in fine condition. The winds chose only the mechanism itself and sucked it up into the vortex which must have hovered just above the barn roof, only to drop the wheel back down into the barn where it now lay, muddy and mangled. The giant hole in the far end of the roof loomed over us. I walked over to Walter to inspect the wheel, but my scrutiny went back to the rope, which now dangled higher above my head. The rafter that held it protruded up through the gap in the roof, as though the storm intended to suck it right out, but had a change of mind. The very top of the rope reached out into the waning light of day and gleamed brightly.

"Look," I pointed out the roof.

"Whoa," Walter interjected, "now that's strange!"

"And there's… the workbench." I hesitated.

"The workbench?"

"The paper said that she stood on a workbench before… " The solid wooden workbench remained in its intended location — shoved up against the sidewall and within reach of the rope before Minnie's body was cut down. Tools that had once been neatly stored on nails above and around it now lay scattered across the dirt floor. Hay settled over everything.

Max's nose led him to unknown parts of the barn.

My mind went into imagining. I knew Minnie did not kill herself. I knew it. She wouldn't do that to me. I talked to her that night, for crying out loud. She sounded fine. We talked about the picnic coming up on Sunday. So that meant that someone hauled her to the barn and hanged her, but I had trouble imagining anyone strong enough to carry a struggling person up onto the top of the workbench to put a rope around her neck.

William was a large man. Surely he was a good six feet tall — with the arms of a man who worked for a living. He wouldn't have had a problem maneuvering any amount of weight if he put his mind to it. He seemed nice enough, but one thing that Phinny's book told me was that impressions can be deceiving. You must dig further to uncover the skeletons. Was William upset that they never had children? Had he been cheating on Minnie? His absences were certainly unusual and poorly timed. Did William see an intimate moment between Marcel and Minnie? There was plenty of evidence to put William to trial, I was sure of it. The big problem was his reputation. William was one of the wealthiest landowners in Clinton County. Everyone knew him. Everyone respected him. People like William were not the recipients of pointed fingers. It was easier to look the other way when someone like him seemed to be guilty. He had too much money to mess around with. That's just the way things were.

I racked my brain about what to do. I was scared. This thing that once seemed like a game steadily proved to be anything but. I knew someone else could easily end up dead. That someone else could be me, Walter, or anyone else I decided to tell. No, I would not tell Mama or Papa what I had been up to. I couldn't put them in danger, too. Papa couldn't do anything anyway. Mama was already beside herself with everything. She wouldn't believe me. The same was true for all my brothers and sisters. No one took me seriously. I was the youngest. Laughable. Cute. No one had any idea who I really was. Not even Christ, who was only a little older than I was. How was it possible to be so alone in such a large family? Minnie was the only one who'd really known me and listened.

"Walter?" I asked.

"Yeah?"

"Do you think he did it?"

"Mr. Seamer?"

"Yes!"

"Well... Mr. Seamer seems kind of guilty to me. He's gone a lot. I know Minnie didn't like it. I know they fought sometimes. He was gone a long time after she died. That seems suspicious to me," Walter acknowledged.

"But... " I encouraged.

"But I have a hard time thinking Mr. Seamer would do such a thing. I've never seen him be mean to anything. He's not like my dad. My dad gets mad at everything, and when he gets that way ... he starts swinging."

"How sure are you that you saw William come home the night she died?" I inquired.

"I'd say 50-50. It sure looked like him, but it was raining. The other weird thing about it was he didn't have his car. He had a horse and cart. Mr. Seamer doesn't even have a cart for traveling anymore. He always drives his car — sometimes rides a horse but not a cart."

"There is a possibility that someone else altogether killed Minnie that night. Maybe Marcel left and whoever was in the cart attacked her," I suggested.

"Naw. I don't think so. If Marcel left, he would have seen whoever was in the cart. He would have said something about that to the sheriff," Walter realized.

"That's true ... unless Marcel is trying to cover up for someone he knows. Maybe he didn't want to get someone in trouble."

"Elsie?" Walter asked.

"Yeah?"

"Do you think it's possible Minnie killed herself? Maybe this is all for nothing."

"Walter!"

"Elsie... the sheriff and those other men looked into it and said it was a suicide. The only people who think she was murdered is you... and partly me."

"No!" I snapped. "You're forgetting something! My father doesn't believe it, either. Remember? I told you about his theory! Minnie's feet were clean! How in the world was she going to walk from the house to the barn in the pouring rain and be completely clean? There was no mud on her!"

"All right, all right," Walter conceded. "I forgot about that part. This is all too complicated for me. I can't keep all this stuff straight."

Walter was sweet, but he was only nine. I felt guilty for losing my temper with him. "Look, Walter... I'm sorry. There's something horrible and dark going on here. I'm not sure I want to figure this all out, but I have to. I have to do it for Minnie. There might be someone else who's in danger, too." I began to pace back and forth.

"We've got to get your notebook back," Walter said. "Then we can keep looking for clues."

"Hey, you two." Both of us jumped. Marcel stood backlit by the setting sun, his frame just a dark shadow. A gorgeous sunset infused the sky with pinks and purples.

"Hey," Walter and I said together.

"What are you doing in here?" Marcel asked.

"Just checking things out," Walter offered.

"The barn's a wreck," I said.

"It's not safe for you to be in here." Marcel forewarned us, "This whole structure is unstable now."

Each of us looked up at the mangled rafters and the rope. Marcel walked closer to us and paused, still looking up at it.

The sun now cast an eerie glow on the part of the rope that protruded from the roof. The remnants of it swayed slightly in the early evening breeze. The barn groaned in protest.

"It's bad, huh?" I offered.

"Sure is. Probably have to tear this barn down and build new," Marcel said.

"Probably you'll want to do that anyway, considering... " Walter guessed.

Marcel nodded. "Your Mama could probably use some help in the house, don't you think?"

I stepped between Walter and Marcel. "Um... we're looking for something." I thought about sharing my thoughts with Marcel again. Now that he had time to think about everything, maybe he was ready to listen.

"What is it?" Marcel asked. "Maybe I can help you."

A shuffle in the doorway brought everyone's attention there. "Are you looking for this?" William stood there, my notebook in his hand. He held it out in front of him, offering it to me. I froze in place and frantically tried to read his expression. Had he read it? I couldn't tell. The only places William had been were the house and the cellar. He'd been inside this whole time. He would have had plenty of time to read everything in it.

Walter and I looked at one another again, both unsure about our next move. Marcel looked from William to us and waited. William stared right at Marcel. The look on his face was blank. I thought, Because of my notebook, were his suspicions about Minnie and Marcel confirmed? What was he thinking? Was this it? Was he going after Marcel now?

"You two kids head back on up to the house. You mentioned you had something else to find." William pointedly fingered a button on his shirt and cocked his head in Marcel's direction. "Now might be a good time," William said to me. A shiver went through me then. It seemed William was encouraging me to go back to look for the shirt the missing button belonged to. I thought he was just trying to get us out of there so he could hurt Marcel.

For an instant, my mind recalled the inner workings of a clock. My Papa tinkered with them in rare moments of free time and loved to show me the intricate wheels and gears that worked together so perfectly. It all seemed inexplicable to me, and I commented on it to my father who assured me that it wasn't at all. "The things that seem random are just puzzles waiting to be solved, Elsie. Sometimes you have to go looking for the pieces that are lost. Once you have all the pieces, even something that looks like chaos turns out to have been order all along."

"Go!" William shouted.

Walter and I broke out in a run. I swiped my notebook from William's outstretched hand as I ran past.

Oh, God! I thought. My panic was fit to burst out of my head. Was William goading me? Did he want me to find the shirt that the

176

missing button belonged to? Or was he sure I would never find it?

To Walter I ordered, "You stay outside and listen for a struggle in the barn. Tell Mama if you hear something! I'm going to check the last of William's shirts."

Thankfully, I did not see Mama as I tore up the stairs and into William's bedroom. I noticed the same shirts hanging there in the closet. The two I hadn't checked were pushed up against the right, and I pulled them simultaneously from the closet. I fully expected to see one missing a button and thought that this would be the sign of a struggle between William and Minnie. This was William's way of telling me I was right, and that I would be the next victim . . . after he took care of Marcel. I thought I saw the spot at first. I expected to see the spot, so I almost made myself see it, even though it wasn't there. It wasn't there! Had William gotten rid of the shirt before I even thought to look?

It dawned on me that maybe William wanted me to look somewhere else. What had he said? *"You mentioned you had something else to find."* Then he felt the button on his shirt but moved his head in Marcel's direction. Was he telling me that the missing button wasn't his at all? Was he telling me the missing button was Marcel's? *"Now might be a good time."*

If the missing button did belong to Marcel, I wasn't sure what that meant but felt a terrible urge to look. I scrambled down the stairs and outside, nearly running into Walter who stared wide-eyed at the barn.

"They're still in there," Walter explained. "I can't tell what they're saying, but they're arguing, that's for sure."

"I need to check Marcel's apartment."

"What for?"

"I just do! Come on!"

We sprinted around the side of the house.

Once inside, the first thing I noticed was the branch that pro-jected through the window on the opposite side of the bedroom. Three feet of a pine branch inserted itself inside and the boughs of it danced with the westerly breeze. Shards of broken glass lit-tered the floor between the window and the foot of Marcel's un-made bed. We walked into the bedroom. A white painted dress-er occupied the wall on our left and various articles of clothing spilled from its drawers. I looked through the shirts littering the floor but found nothing, so I checked the dresser. On my way over to it, my foot struck a plate peeking out from under the bed, and it skittered across the floor. I jumped and Walter swore.

I rifled through each drawer in turn.

Drawer one: Grey socks. Long johns and underwear. Magazines that featured half-clothed women.

Drawer two: Work pants and a penny.

Drawer three: Work shirts. One blue. One grey.

My hands trembled as I picked up the grey shirt. The right sleeve had several brown stains that could have been… blood. Discern-ibly missing from the shirt was one grey button. I held my breath as I felt around inside my dress pocket for the button I found underneath Minnie's bed. I brought it out, and as realization dawned, my trembling hands dropped it promptly; then it rolled across the floor and into the mess of broken glass.

"I got it!" Walter assured me.

"Don't cut yourself again!"

He picked his way through the glass and around the jutting tree branch. "Here!"

Taking the button from Walter, I held it in its original place on the shirt and made my final decision on the matter. Unmistakable, I decided. This was the shirt. What did this mean? Were Minnie and Marcel locked in a passionate embrace? In their haste did a button pop from his shirt? Was this William's way of showing me that Minnie and Marcel were having an affair? Surely the dried blood was explainable. I'd seen earlier that day one of the many jobs Marcel had around the farm involving blood.

While these thoughts churned in my head, my eyes darted around the room. Marcel's narrow bed, along with a small nightstand, was pushed up against the wall on our right, just beyond an unbroken window. An empty coffee cup and a drained J.F. Cutter whiskey bottle were the only objects on it. I walked over to the bottle and picked it up.

"What is it? What's going on, Elsie?"

My heart pumped so hard it hurt. "Oh, no," I mumbled, "oh, no."

This was without a doubt the same type of bottle that Christ found at my brother's house. The large star in the center was unmistakable. Bottle, button, bottle, button. Marcel was the last known person with Minnie before she died.

"Elsie!" Walter began to feel panicky. "Tell me!"

My mind reeled. "Marcel… What if her killer is Marcel?"

I heard a noise from behind. Footsteps on Marcel's porch. I dropped the shirt on the floor, shoved the button back in my pocket, and scrambled for the unbroken window. Walter was already there, yanking up on the window frame with all his strength. I hastily stepped beside him and we pulled together for a second before I realized that the window was securely painted shut.

"Under the bed!" I whispered. It was the only place to go, so both Walter and I squirmed under and held our breath. Our heads were underneath the foot of it, closest to the dresser. The bed-clothes had not been made, so we could see out the bedroom all the way through to the porch door. It was a help and a hurt, for surely someone could see us with little trouble at all.

The door opened. Marcel's brown work boots clumped across the hardwood floor. I spotted something else just then. Something that sent a terror through me more thoroughly than anything ever did before. Dangling from Marcel's hand was a freshly bloodied axe handle. That could only mean one thing. I turned my head to face Walter. Clearly, he saw it, too. His eyes were big and he bit his lower lip.

I squeezed my eyes shut tight as Marcel's footsteps echoed menacingly in the bedroom. My hands curled up into little balls next to my head, and my throat let out an involuntary whimper. Walter reached out for my hand and we clutched each other tightly. Marcel walked over to his dresser where we heard him set down the handle. Then he reached down and picked up the shirt I'd dropped on the floor. A few seconds later, he walked over to the nightstand, opened a drawer, rummaged about inside, and slowly shut it back up again.

"Elsie, Walter, I know you're in here. Come on out."

Both Walter and I were much too frightened to move — like rabbits freeze when they know a predator is near. They hope beyond hope that if they stay perfectly still, they won't be noticed. I wondered if we just stayed quiet enough, would Marcel assume we really were not in there at all?

I heard his knee crack as Marcel crouched down and peered under the bed. Walter and I stared at his dark eyes for a moment. No discernable emotion crossed his face. "Come on, now, get out," he coaxed.

I refused to get out on the side of the bed closest to Marcel, so I motioned for Walter to scooch out on the side farthest from him. We emerged through the broken glass just next to the shattered window. The protruding branch and the bed served as barriers between us and Marcel. We stood up to face him.

"Why are you looking through my things?" he asked, while holding out the grey shirt. "What are you hoping to find?"

My eyes quickly glanced at the reddened axe handle sitting on top of Marcel's dresser. He watched me look there and still betrayed no emotion.

"I've already found it," I remarked boldly. Poor Walter stood frozen in place, not making a sound.

"What did you find?" Marcel asked.

The puzzle was almost complete, but this time I neared the finish reluctantly. My voice shook. "Is that the shirt you were wearing when Minnie died?" The stained sleeve brushed the floorboards.

"Elsie, I think this little investigation of yours has gone to your head. You're acting crazy, and you're causing those around you to act that way, too."

"I'm not crazy," I said.

Marcel countered, "I just had a very interesting conversation with Mr. Seamer. Thanks to that notebook of yours, he seems to think I had something to do with Minnie's death, too. It's simply not true. Surely you don't think I'd be capable of something like that?"

I dropped my eyes to the floor, still wondering, despite the evidence, despite the bloodied handle just feet away from us.

A squeak managed its way from Walter's throat. "Wha... Wha... What have you done to Mr. Seamer?"

"Nothing he didn't have coming to him. Don't you see? It was William all along. You were right, Elsie. The last time you came to my apartment and told me you thought William may have killed Minnie, and that I might be next? You were right. He just attacked me out there. Came after me with a crow bar!" Marcel shook his head in disbelief and dropped the shirt he'd been holding.

Walter managed, "Is... is he dead?"

Marcel smiled and slowly nodded his head.

"I don't believe you!" Walter managed. Tears streamed down his face.

"Now, I don't know what sorts of things you've written in that book of yours," — without thinking, my right hand felt the pocket where my notebook lay — "but I'm going to need it." Marcel walked over to the bed until his knees just touched it. His one hand remained at his side. "And if you want to leave this room, you're going to give it to me, right now!" His voice rose ever so slightly, forsaking his calm demeanor.

"Why do you want it so bad, if William is the one who killed her?" I asked.

"You've already convinced William that I did it; if you still want to convince others, I'm going to have to do something drastic," he threatened.

I reached out for Walter's trembling hand.

"I'm not afraid of you!" I challenged.

"Elsie . . . this isn't just about you any more. This is about your friend Walter and your mother and father. Unless you want to involve them even more, you'd better hand it over. Don't make me do something you'll regret. You can hand over the notebook right now, and we'll forget any of this ever happened."

The robins and finches flitted about confidently now. They mingled among the bushes just outside the open window. The birds called my attention to the only way out I could see at the time. I yanked the notebook from my pocket and sent it sailing right out the damaged window and onto the littered yard beyond.

"I won't be silent about the things I know. Not any more!" I warned.

"You stupid, stubborn girl!" Marcel said coolly. With that, he shoved the bed with his knees right into us and pinned us up against the wall. Walter and I screamed bloody murder.

With the back of his hand, Marcel struck Walter in the face, and my eyes detected a flash of something silver clutched by his thumb. Walter slumped over onto the bed and didn't move. I continued screaming.

Marcel's hand streaked close to my neck, and he stopped. The silver object was a straight razor, and it was poised right at my throat. I quit screaming and my eyes alternated between Marcel's deep brown eyes and the cutting edge of the instrument.

"I trusted you," I whimpered. "I trusted you!" Hot tears of anger and shame streamed down my face.

"It's too bad it has to end this way, Elsie. I do like you." I let out a whimper but could not bring myself to scream again. I knew if I did, I would be dead. The razor cut a thin line of flesh and a trickle of blood slid down my neck and into the hollow of my throat. "You want to know what happened to your sister? This is what happened."

Suddenly, he tossed the razor onto the floor behind us. I tried to scream again, but was halted by the force of his hand as it snapped back and seized my throat.

Was this how Minnie died? Was she choked to death? I braced my right hand around Marcel's wrist and used my left to try to pry away his bullish fingers. They didn't budge.

"It's impossible to hide the bruising this leaves behind. Suicide by hanging is the only other way to explain it. Fire is, of course, another useful distraction." He squeezed even harder.

I closed my eyes and tried with all my might to save myself. Seconds passed and bursts of color sprang up inside my clenched eyelids. I began to fade.

"I thought we had something . . . Minnie and I. I shared things with her, but she turned out to be like all the rest."

With my own life leaving me, I knew how it happened. My dream didn't take me any further, for I heard something more real just then. More concrete than my sister's screams. More absolute than Marcel's grunts as he moved her body out to the barn. More evident than the cries of the horses in my brother's barn. Shrieks. My mother! And shouts. Then I heard the authoritative sound of death.

January 1913

A few hours after I fell asleep tonight, William woke me upon his return from Clinton. He crawled into bed, held my shoulders in his broad hands, and whispered, "Wake up, Minnie. I've got something to show you." I trembled at the tickle in my ear and the shiver that traveled down my spine. Dumb with sleep I rose and fumbled my way into the long wool coat William held out for me and worked gently over my shoulders. Then he offered my hat and gloves, "It's very cold out there." I was afraid to ask what we were about to see. I couldn't read his expression in the vague white light bouncing off the snow through my frost-covered windows, but William held my hand down the groaning stairs, and I sensed a boyhood wonder in him that comforted me.

We stepped away from the house and crunched our way over the hard-packed snow. We broke through the towering evergreens in the front yard and into the open space near the road. I checked his face for some direction or explanation. His thumb and forefinger directed my gaze while raising my chin to the rare and magical beauty of the Northern Lights dancing over our heads. I'd only read about them, but there they were — waltzing to and fro right over Iowa. I didn't know such a thing was possible here. Thank you, husband.

Self – Defense

Expect to get into dangerous situations. What should you do when you have to protect yourself?

Moon Shadow

Moon peers through the shadows of night and cloud
Some company in light:
Stars
Fireflies
Planets
The eyes of the living
Stealthy the spirits of the dead
Composed now
And fit for departure

From far away — shouts. The choking pressure on my neck abruptly stopped, and I collapsed onto the bed. Life asserted itself from a distant place. Sounds were muffled as if I had a stack of pillows over my head. The pain in my neck flashed and deepened. It sounded like Mama far off, maybe shouting my name from Minnie's living room, but I thought I felt her rough hands on my arms and stroking my hair. A thump from somewhere. After a time, my feet were raised up and onto something soft. Then I saw streams of light through my closed eyelids as my body turned over. Mama said my name over and over again. The world was like this for untold moments in time. Forever or an hour.

Gradually, my eyes opened, and Mama gazed down into my face. Her lips silently formed a prayer of thanks and she kissed me on my forehead. "Can you sit?" I nodded my head as the reality of all that just happened washed over me. Was Walter okay? Where was Marcel? The pain in my neck was unbearable.

William sat next to the wall by the door. One of his hands held a bloody cloth to his skull. He looked at me and said, "He won't be bothering you again, Elsie. He won't be bothering anybody ever again." William's eyes traveled from me, down to the floor near the bed. I looked around my mother.

Marcel lay on his side, eyes open, and blood trickled from his mouth and dripped on the rug — the tines of a pitchfork thrust deeply into his torso. I shuddered as I watched the rug slowly become more and more saturated with the oozing blood. The straight razor he had held to my neck still lay on the floor, far from the dead man's reach.

Walter still lay slumped over on the bed but slowly began to stir as Mama rubbed his hair and back. "Elsie… " he murmured.

"I'm here … " was all I could manage; I coughed uncontrollably for a minute as my throat got used to breathing and talking again. I reached out for Walter's hand and squeezed. He raised his head up and I saw a deep, dark bruise plume over his right eye and down the side of his face.

"You stay right there, Walter. I'll get you a cool rag for that eye," Mama promised. Careful to step around the bloodied rug, she bustled out to the kitchen where I heard her pumping water. Walter worked his way into a sitting position on the bed and leaned his back up against the wall. I watched him regard William and gasp at the figure of Marcel's bleeding body. The blood continued flowing toward the edges of the rug. Mama came back in and handed Walter a wet rag.

"Hold this to your eye now," she instructed.

Walter moaned as he gently pressed the cold rag to his face.

"We'd better see to that wound of yours now, William." Mama went back to the kitchen and returned with a bucket of water and clean rags. She knelt down next to him and pulled his hands away from his bleeding head. William held no form of protest. He just stared at the wall while her shaking hands dabbed at the gash, ripped a towel into strips, and bandaged his head. The bleeding slowed considerably, but blood still seeped into the cloth.

When finished, Mama lifted her large frame up off the floor and sat at the foot of the bed with Walter and me. She let out a long sigh. "Now, someone had better tell me what happened here. All I know is I heard screams. When I finally figured out where the screams were coming from, Marcel had a pitchfork in him, and you two were lying on the bed."

My throat was not fit for talking just yet. William didn't speak a word — just continued to stare at the wall.

Walter volunteered, "Mrs. Edens! Marcel killed Minnie! And he tried to kill us, too!"

"What?" Mama looked from William to me, looking for confirmation. I nodded my head.

"It's true," William managed. "I found Elsie's notebook in the cellar. Elsie's been taking notes on her suspicions about Minnie's death. She suspected me of killing her, but some of the things that she uncovered made me realize that Marcel may have had something to do with her death. I went to the barn to confront him about it. We exchanged words. He surprised me with that axe handle."

"Why would he do such a thing?" Mama slowly shook her head.

"I could have stopped him. I saw them . . . through the window that night," William admitted.

"That *was* you!" Walter cried.

"What do you mean, you saw them?" Mama asked.

"Minnie and Marcel kissing. In our living room."

"Are you sure?"

"I'm sure," William said, defeated.

"But Minnie must've tried to stop him!" Walter offered. "That's when . . . " he trailed off.

"It's true," I coughed and cleared my throat. The ability to speak and breathe was painful, but I couldn't stay quiet any longer. I pulled the button from my pocket and rose off the bed to retrieve the grey shirt from Marcel's floor. "I found this button under Minnie's bed." I showed Mama the shirt as I held the button in place.

"Surely a button doesn't prove Marcel is guilty of such a thing,"

Mama said in disbelief.

That was when I showed her the brown stains on the right sleeve. Mama had seen plenty of bloodstains on clothing through the years. She knew what she was looking at. "Those stains could be Marcel's own blood or from Lord knows what. I don't think... "

"Then there's the bottle, Elsie! Tell her about the bottle."

"What bottle?" Mama questioned.

I walked over to the empty whiskey bottle, which now lay cracked and broken on the floor. I pointed. "When Christ and I picked up at John and Nell's the other day, he found a whiskey bottle like this one in the barn rubble, Mama."

"Oh, for heaven's sake, he was probably there helping to put out the fire," Mama scolded.

"Nell mentioned that she didn't see Marcel at the fire that night, but he was there all right," I said. "He started it."

A slow, reluctant realization dawned all over Mama's face as she pieced together what must have happened. "Papa said that Minnie's feet were clean... That someone must have carried her. I thought that maybe... I just thought Papa was crazy."

"We were all fooled," William muttered.

"Elsie, if you knew all this, why didn't you tell us?" Mama asked.

"I didn't know for sure who did it. Until today. I only suspected. I thought you would all think I was crazy. I'm just a kid. I didn't think you'd believe me. I was looking for proof." I stopped.

Mama reached out for my hand. "And that's why he hurt you? Because you knew?"

I nodded. "When he was choking me . . . he told me that that was how he did it, Mama. That he choked her and hanged her to hide the bruises."

Mama stared out the window, silent for a while.

Walter filled her in on the things that happened that day, starting with me losing my notebook. While he talked, I walked outside and retrieved it. Darkness now took over the land, but the moon shone just enough to help me find my notebook. The gander, now back but still alone, hesitantly called out for his flock from under the willow tree.

When I came back inside, I saw tears trickle down William's face. I sat down beside him and he said, "All this time . . . all this time I thought she killed herself because she hated me. I thought she knew about . . . " William lowered his head. "I did love her."

"It's time to call the sheriff," Mama decided. Then she left the room.

Slowly the three of us started for the door. I stared down at Marcel's body and shivered. Cracks in the wooden floor drew in his blood as the carpet could take on no more. Walter and I had to leap over it so as not to get any on our shoes.

* * * * *

We waited for Sheriff Dohgherty back over at William's side of the house. Walter and I sat at the kitchen table. Mama gave us some corn bread with syrup, but neither one of us could eat it. William lay on his sofa after Mama re-bandaged his head. The wound couldn't seem to stop oozing blood. All was quiet, except for the sounds of Mama walking upstairs. She'd gone up to check on Papa. I wondered if he was aware enough to be filled in on what happened, or if Mama would even want to tell him. I knew she was worried about putting any more stress on him, espe-

192

cially after the already trying day.

I had a vague idea what time it was; the clock in Minnie's kitchen still didn't work. After maybe an hour or so of sitting in the kitchen, we heard the low rumble of the sheriff's car as it pulled into the drive. The headlights streamed across the house and peeked in on the kitchen for a moment before winking out. Mama creaked down the stairs. Black circles pooled under her eyes. I'd never seen her look so tired.

William sat up and rose to meet the sheriff at the door. "I got a call, Will. What's going on?"

"That was me, sheriff," Mama said. "You take him on over, William; I'll stay here with the children."

William nodded and walked out past the sheriff who glanced at us and left. They were gone maybe a half hour before returning. Walter was half asleep, his chin in his hands. The banging of the screen door woke him back up.

"I'm sorry, everyone. I know you've had a long night, and it hasn't been easy, but I'm going to have to ask everybody a few questions," the sheriff apologized.

And so the sheriff talked to each one of us in turn. First Mama, then me, then Walter. He walked us each out to the porch where we got to tell our side of the story. When he and Walter came back inside, the sheriff turned to Mama, "Does your husband know about all this, Mrs. Edens?"

"He does, sheriff. My husband's a sick man, but much more aware of things than I gave him credit for. I've told him everything I know."

"Then we'd better head on upstairs for what I've got to say next. He'll need to hear it, too," the sheriff informed us.

Each of us trudged upstairs to Papa's room. My bones sagged in my torso like a sack of potatoes. It was all I could do to put one foot in front of the other. I teetered a bit as I got to the top of the steps, and William placed his hand between my shoulders to steady me.

Father was awake. He breathed shallowly, and his sad eyes met mine as we walked through the door. I walked over to him and grasped his hand. His fever seemed to have lowered a bit. He motioned for me to sit on the bed.

"Well, everyone, what I've got to say is a bit unorthodox, but... Are you sure about this, Will?" the sheriff asked.

"I don't have anything to hide anymore, Warren. Not from them."

"Then maybe you'd better start by telling them what you told me the day after Minnie died. They'll need to know."

William nodded his head as all eyes turned toward him. Walter slumped against a wall. Mama sat down in the chair next to Papa's bed. William began.

"Things hadn't been so good for us since the baby died. Real bad, in fact. She was a different woman — I didn't know her anymore." William paused.

"Keep going... " the sheriff encouraged.

"We fought a lot, but a person can only put up with that for so long. I began to spend more and more time away. I hoped that one day I would come back and she would be her old self again. I didn't stay away long; I'd go for the weekend to buy cattle, only instead of going once a month as I used to do, I went every weekend. He paused and gazed out the window. The sheriff cleared his throat.

"The day she died, we had another fight. I planned to leave for Rock Island Friday, and come home sometime Saturday afternoon. By then, the cattle auction would be over. She brought up the idea of attending the picnic out at John's place on Sunday. I suppose I was feeling cross, because I told her that I didn't want to go, but I asked her if she would like to come with *me*. I thought it would do her some good to get out of the house. She just scoffed at me and walked away. So I left."

"Keep going," said the sheriff. "They'll need to know what happened that day to cause the rest of it to make sense."

William hesitated, clutching his head in his hands, and winced in pain.

"My next stop was the garage in Clinton. I'd an appointment to get a tube replaced and have the oil checked and such. I told them I'd be back by noon to pick it up. From there my plan was to go straight to Rock Island. Auctions generally started around 3 p.m. on Friday afternoons and reconvened Saturday mornings. By then I had a standing reservation at a small hotel that served supper to me. It had become a welcome routine.

"While I waited for the car to get done, my plan was to hold up at the feed store. The boys always gathered there for talk and coffee, and I thought it would be a good way to spend the morning. I'd even told them to expect me, as I had to wait for the garage to be done with the auto.

"But... I don't know. I guess I didn't feel much like talking to the boys after fighting with Minnie. So I found some place on 2nd Street. I thought, a couple of drinks and I'd be on my way.

"I wonder if I'd just gone to the feed store if things would have turned out differently because I wouldn't have been drunk. Maybe Minnie would still be alive. When I saw them, what I should have done was confront him — not leave. I *left* her. I *left* her."

"What did you see, William?" Mama asked. She clutched the folds of her dress and twisted and worried them about in her hands.

"He'll have to warm up to that, Mrs. Edens," the sheriff explained.

"So a couple of drinks turned to several, and several drinks turned into... a lot. Then an old friend wandered in. He'd been my best friend when we were boys. We shared more drinks and played a few games of cards with some of the other men, but at the same time, the fight with Minnie wasn't far from my thoughts.

"After a while, I told Matt I needed to go. I'd made up my mind that I had to get back home — talk to Minnie and sort out this thing that was happening between us. I half ran back to the garage, and on the way I picked up a small bouquet of flowers for her; irises were her favorite. When I got to the garage and tried the door, it was locked. They were closed. I couldn't believe it! I'd wasted away an entire day and now couldn't get my car. I thought about hopping the train to Low Moor. Elvira was only four miles from there. I could walk that, but I wondered if it was worth it. I imagined going through all that trouble only to have Minnie brush me off and lock herself in the bedroom.

"Back at the bar I told Matt of my predicament. He offered me an out. He planned on staying on in Clinton all night. The 2nd Street brothels were calling to him, and he thought he'd find a place to stay, so he wouldn't have to ride home after dark. The new moon would offer no light to him, and he thought he could use a night of women and booze. He let me take his cart back to Elvira as long as I met him at his place in the morning. He'd pick up my car at the garage, and meet me there at 7:30. I could leave from there to attend the Saturday auctions in Rock Island. It sounded like a good plan to me. I accepted. I felt a desperate urge to get back home then. My obstacles only made me more determined.

"The ride home was wet. Occasional lightning lit up the sky. Matt's poor horse was miserable, and I sure as heck was. The

196

flowers I bought earlier I abandoned in the ditch not far from here; they were ruined in the rain."

William trailed off again. Each of us adjusted ourselves in our seats, impatient and frightened of the rest of the story all at the same time.

"The light coming from the living room windows was just about the most inviting thing I'd ever seen. I knew Minnie was in there — probably listening to music and writing letters or sewing. I imagined going on in, soaking wet. Minnie would scold me for getting water all over the floor; I would stop her with a kiss, sweep her off her feet, and we would go on upstairs. All would be forgiven. If only…

"I directed the horse to the barn to bed down for the night, but my position in the carriage allowed me to see right into the living room and happen upon a scene that changed everything. Minnie and Marcel were locked in an embrace on the couch."

"Oh, no, Minnie!" Mama groaned.

"Then Marcel leaned in to kiss her. Minnie did not push him away. Anger welled up inside of me, but something else did, too. Was it me? I thought. Was there something wrong with me? Did Minnie think so, too? I couldn't bring myself to storm in on that scene. I would only want to knock Marcel into kingdom come. I couldn't blame him for liking her. She was a beautiful woman, and she was hurting. Something was wrong; I couldn't fix it. Maybe he could. It was worth allowing her some comfort to see her be her old self again.

"I turned the horse toward Low Moor where I spent the night at Matt's. His place was not strange to me; before marrying Minnie I'd stayed there many times after a long night. I knew he wouldn't mind, and I'd still have his horse there in the morning, as promised.

"I didn't sleep much that night — I wondered what else went on between Minnie and Marcel, and a thousand things played through my mind.

"Morning came, but not Matt. I gave some thought to going back home instead but decided to stick with my plan. If I went home now, I knew Minnie and I would fight. Matt promised to meet me by 7:30, so I could leave for the auctions. By 8:30 he still hadn't come, so I decided to walk the half-mile to the train station and take the train to Davenport. From there I could catch another train to Rock Island and still be in time for the auction. Catching a train back to Clinton would be no problem. I figured I'd check to see if my car was still at the garage — maybe Matt had run into a problem, and they wouldn't release it to him. If it wasn't there, I'd just hop the train back to Low Moor and get it. Either way, I'd be back home when I originally said I would be. Then I'd see about sorting things out. I'd see what I could do to make things right between us again.

"When I got back and found out that Minnie was dead, I . . . I couldn't believe that she killed herself, but considering how different she was since the baby died and all, I let myself believe it. I had to make peace with her death somehow, so I convinced myself that Minnie was a different person. My Minnie wouldn't have done that; my Minnie wouldn't have kissed Marcel Masters, either. I assumed that she killed herself out of depression and shame. I assumed she hated me. I couldn't reveal that I came home and saw her with Marcel. I needed to protect her honor as much as possible; it was bad enough that she killed herself. I couldn't damage her honor further by revealing the affair, too."

William stared out the dark window. Everyone was silent for a moment until the sheriff said, "You all know Will and I are friends. Have been since we were kids. But I still needed to follow up on Will's whereabouts and verify that this story was correct. I did… to a point. I didn't ask Marcel about having an affair with Minnie. I knew if I did, the papers would find out about it, and the one thing Will wanted that I could give him was protecting Minnie's reputation as much as possible. It seemed clear that she committed suicide. That was scandal enough. The two of us agreed to keep our knowledge of that quiet. Even from Marcel himself."

The sheriff continued, "If we reopen the investigation of Minnie's death, Minnie's involvement with Marcel will come out."

"What do you mean, *if* you reopen the investigation?" Mama asked, hand on her hip. "My daughter was murdered! Everyone thinks she killed herself! If I can protect her from *this* kind of reputation, I will!"

My father began to cough as he attempted to speak. Mama warned, "You need to rest, Christ, I'll take care of this."

"No . . . " father protested weakly, and he loosened my grip from his hand. "I would rather . . . that people think of Minnie as a woman . . . who committed suicide than one who was unfaithful, taken advantage of, and murdered." He coughed long and hard. Mama held a handkerchief to his mouth, and spatters of blood stained it. After he recovered, he resumed. "Everyone knows how upset she was after the baby died. People can sympathize with that. I'll not have them think of her as an adulteress who got in over her head."

"You can't possibly . . . " Mama started.

"If the sheriff is willing . . . " Papa coughed again. Then he turned and looked directly at William. "You avenged my daughter's death. I know you loved her. How could you not? The murderer is dead. Sheriff . . . what do you propose?"

Mama looked in disbelief from Papa to the sheriff. "The children need to get to bed. I'll not have them hear of such things."

"They'll stay!" Papa asserted weakly. It looked like it hurt him to talk. "If it weren't for Elsie we would be none the wiser." He looked at the sheriff and waited for him to answer.

"Does Marcel have any family to speak of?" The sheriff asked.

"No. At least he didn't talk of any. Said he was from out East. Never got any calls or letters from family that I know about," William offered.

"Well, the way I see it — you've got two choices. Damage Minnie's reputation by opening the case all over again. Open Will up to possible conviction over Marcel's death, or leave things be as they are now and quietly get rid of the body. Hired men move on all the time. The thing is, you'll all need to agree on a course of action here." The sheriff looked at each of us in turn and waited for an answer.

"Hide it. Protect Minnie," Papa voted.

"Do you mean it's possible William could go to jail over this?" Mama asked.

"It's possible. Anytime you hand over a case like this to a jury, you never know. There's been some talk of Will's guilt in town. Gossip over his whereabouts and what not. Some suspect visits to 2nd street, and I'm not just talking about the bars. Stories are going around. I wouldn't put it past the prosecutor to concoct a wild story that links Will to both deaths. Buttons and bottles are hardly evidence."

"But he tried to kill Elsie and… " Mama asserted.

"That doesn't prove that he killed Minnie. It could be said that he simply tried to suppress Elsie's story by scaring her. That even though he didn't do it, he was afraid people would think so. A good prosecutor can spin this in a lot of believable ways, and

Clinton County has a good prosecutor. The man has no regard for someone's reputation, only conviction."

"He confessed to Elsie!" Mama reminded the sheriff.

"He confessed to a young girl who passed out. Not a reliable witness. Protect the innocent or protect the guilty, ma'am. That's the way I see it."

Walter nodded his head and rubbed his eyes.

Mama slumped down deeper into her chair, defeated. "We can't just hide Marcel's body here. The whole town's going to know," she pointed out.

Everyone mulled that over. The room was deathly quiet. I imagined Minnie's ghost hovering over us, waiting for the answer. I saw her smile — content with the events of the night, her death avenged. "I know a good place!" I decided. "They buried all the horses at John's when Christ and I were there!"

"That's ridiculous, Elsie!" Mama asserted.

"But it's a really big hole, Mama. Freshly dug."

"Actually," the sheriff confirmed, "I can't think of a better place."

"Do it," Papa said, his head slumped deeper into the pillow, exhausted.

William nodded his head.

"We have to be sure that no one is going to talk about what they know. The papers published the truth as far as anyone here is concerned. As long as you're alive, you need to keep this to yourself," the sheriff pointed out.

"I won't say anything!" I assured him.

"I won't either," confirmed Walter.

I stared at his black and blue eye. "What about your eye, Walter? What will your parents say?"

Walter thought for a minute and lowered his head. "My dad will probably think he did it when he was drunk. My Ma will be too afraid to say anything."

Mama walked over to Walter and squeezed his shoulder. Then she looked up at William and the sheriff and said, "I'll call John and tell him to expect you."

"Be careful what you say over the phone, Mrs. Edens," the sheriff warned. "You never know who's listening." Back then, the operator could hear every word if she wanted to listen in.

"Don't you worry about that. I know how to be discreet," Mama assured him. "Now Walter, you head on home. It's awful late. If your parents get upset with you, tell them to call here. Tell them William asked for your help cleaning up the place."

Walter looked gratefully up at my mother, smiled back at me, and ran down the stairs.

Papa held out his hand to mother who walked over to him. She grasped his palm and they exchanged a silent look. Mama left the room. William and the sheriff followed after her.

"I'm proud of you, Elsie," Papa said to me. I laid my head down on his chest, but not for long. I could hear death rattling around in there, and it frightened me. "You go along now. I need rest."

"Thank you, Papa." I kissed him on the cheek and left the room.

Back in Minnie's kitchen, Mama waited for the operator to connect her with my brother John while William and the sheriff waited beside her.

"John? Yes, it's me... No, it's not about your father... It's, well, William and Elsie are headed your way. Be prepared to receive them. They can explain everything; Elsie will speak for me. What she says is best for the family. Just know that... No, that's all I can say now. I'll speak with you tomorrow... yes... good night."

Moments later, I watched out the window as the sheriff pulled a large tarp from his car and laid it in William's back seat. His car had been pulled up close to the house. Then the two men carried out Marcel's body. They had rolled it up in the soaked rug and now placed it on top of the tarp. Afterward, William led him over to the water pump where they washed their bloody hands.

"You'll need to go with William, Elsie," Mama informed me. "I've got to stay with your father. John will need an explanation and you're the one to give it to him. He'll believe you."

I nodded my head. Mama let out a small sigh. "Don't worry, Mama. The sheriff's right. We have to protect the innocent people. Marcel was a bad man. He deserved it. Do you remember when you told me that those in hell can't be helped by prayer, and those in heaven have no need of our prayers? No matter what we pray, no matter what we say, or don't say, or do, or don't do, Minnie will be in heaven. And Marcel will be in hell."

Mama and I hugged then. It was the first real hug I'd shared with her since I was a very small child. We held each other for a long time before the sheriff poked his head in the door. "It's time, Elsie."

I looked up at her, and she looked down at me. "Get some rest, Mama. You deserve it."

The sheriff walked me out to William's car. "I'll not be going, Elsie. You and Will can handle this on your own. You're a brave girl. And a smart one. Maybe when you get old enough you can come work in the sheriff's department. I could use a good office girl."

I thought for a minute. "I don't think so, sheriff. I've plans to become a private investigator. I've sort of already taken my first class."

He chuckled a bit and said, "I've no doubt you can make that happen if you have a mind to." Then he nodded his head at Will and left.

* * * * *

The ride over to John's was short. He lived less than two miles away, but every moment drew itself out like a dream. Unbearably close was the smell of blood in the back seat. Marcel's ghost loomed over me like a nightmarish menace. My neck throbbed and I felt his hand around my throat all over again. I sank down in the seat as far as I dared lest William think I was scared. The sounds of countless crickets and small tree frogs filled my ears as they rang out their calls to one another in anxious attempts at companionship before the dawn. A family of raccoons lumbered their way across the road as William slowed down to miss them.

"I'm sorry you got involved in all of this, Elsie," William said.

I wasn't sure what to say to that, so I just muttered, "That's okay."

"But I'm glad you did."

I knew what he meant. He knew now. Minnie didn't kill herself. She saw some hope ahead of her. She didn't hate him, after all.

The pungent smell of fresh-cut hay filled the car as we neared John's place — that, and still the smell of burnt wood. My nose wasn't sure what to think of all the strong smells assaulting it. My stomach felt queasy, and I longed for some of Mama's strong mint tea to make me feel right again. Only I don't think any amount of tea could have made me feel quite the same. I can smell the blood and the burn right now as I'm telling you this. It's the worst combination I can think of.

William and I walked up to John who stood under the porch light. Dozens of white moths flew a precarious path toward its beam.

"Evening," John greeted us.

"Nell here?" William asked.

"Naw. Drove her into Davenport this morning to stay with her sick mother for a few days."

"That's probably best," William said.

"What's going on?"

It took us a good half hour of talk to get it all out and answer any questions John had. We sat on the edges of his porch and listened to the night sounds ebb and flow around the horror of our story. Sitting made me feel sleepy all over again, and I found myself trying to gauge the time. I thought it might be midnight.

"You've got him in your car right now?" John asked, in disbelief.

"Right in there," I pointed out.
"Then let's bury the murdering bastard."

William and I sighed and my shoulders fell in relief.

As the slivered moon and two kerosene lamps lit our way, the sounds of three shovels worked in harmony. The earth welcomed the effort; digging was easy. We dug as far down as we could while avoiding the carcasses of the dead horses. William and John grunted as they pulled Marcel's body from the back seat of the car — tarp, rug, and all. "One, two..." John said as they swung it back and forth. Just before they let the body go into the hole, I shouted, "Wait!" William dropped his end in exhaustion and loose strands of Marcel's dark hair poked out from the end of the rolled fabric. I hastened over to it and pulled back the tarp and saturated rug, so I could see him. His eyes were still open. Then I gathered what spit I could and spattered it all over his cursed face.

April 1913

William seems to be coming back to me now. I've changed over the months — back into some semblance of who I was before. We are trying to rebuild this life together. The effort consists of stops and starts. Some days it is ugly, and other days it is nothing short of beautiful. I do love him, and I believe he loves me.

I invited Elsie to come stay with us finally. I introduced her to Walter and he showed her around the farm. (There have been many changes to our livestock and buildings since she was here last.) It is almost a completely different place. Or, maybe, it is just me who has changed. Anyway, we had a wonderful time together. She is a sister, but her age makes her feel more like a daughter to me. I wonder what Mama would think if Elsie were to stay with me for the summer? She helps out quite a bit at the hotel; she must be thirteen now? I know I missed her last birthday. No one bothered to ask me; everyone knew I was in no shape to celebrate it. I'll have to make that up to her.

I learned something last night. Marcel and William came in from checking the cattle; William was in the barn and Marcel crouched at the water pump soaking his head. I walked over there to fill up the watering can and stood waiting. I flushed in embarrassment as he stood, for Marcel was naked from the waist up and I found myself staring at the mangled looking scar where his arm used to be. He commented that I was blushing which was true. I apologized, and he said he didn't mind me looking. I wasn't sure what to make of that, so I moved to fill up the bucket. Then he asked if I wanted to know what happened to his arm. This was a shock, for numerous times we have tripped around the subject. He has made it quite clear in the past that this was something he did not want to discuss. I told him that if he was ready to tell me, I was ready to listen. There was a moment's pause as if Marcel was weighing whether or not to tell me the whole truth, but I've no doubt he did, for the story is downright horrible.

Apparently he was accused of some wrongdoing against a young girl many counties away. He was declared not guilty by the authorities, but the brother of the girl didn't believe the verdict.

This brother, along with a few of his friends, hauled Marcel down to the railroad tracks where they beat him and tied him up somehow. The train ran over his arm, severing it from his body as sure as anything. The brother and the friends took off running, but others were alerted to Marcel's screams and ran to help. The local doctor was able to save him, but barely. He wasn't altogether clear about the nature of the accusation, but I can guess. If the powers that be found him innocent though, who am I to judge? Marcel hasn't done a thing to show me that he is anything but honorable. That he chose to share this with me shows that he trusts me, and this warms me to him.

May 1913

Marcel's apartment is separate from ours in every way. He has his own entrance and stairs to the second floor as well as his own kitchen and sitting room. So it will come as a surprise to say that Marcel caught me in a compromising position yesterday. The heat in the house was unbearable. May is as unpredictable as Iowa can get. Just last week I wore a shawl out to hang clothes on the line, and now any bit of clothing is too much. So to get to the point, I stood over the basin in the kitchen and unbuttoned my blouse. Taking a cool, wet rag I refreshed myself so as not to faint from the heat. I dabbed my forehead and face as well. When I looked up, Marcel stood in the entrance, staring at me. He should have excused himself right away and left, but he did not. He stood there. I assured him this was not appropriate as I buttoned up my blouse. A smile crept over his lips. Then he tipped his hat at me and left. Despite the heat, a shiver ran down my spine.

The Bigger Picture

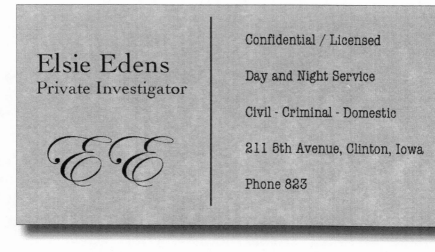

Confidential / Licensed

Day and Night Service

Civil - Criminal - Domestic

211 5th Avenue, Clinton, Iowa

Phone 823

Elsie Edens
Private Investigator

Yours is one perspective. Keep looking for more. What is your purpose?

A Requited Love

The burgeoning moon
Revealed a shimmering specter before me
She disappeared from momentary view
Only to reappear yards later
Unperturbed and on a sure path
Through dark ditch grasses and fireflies
A perfect bouquet of flowers
Called out to her and she knelt to receive it
Forgotten love, renewed.

There are two different kinds of signs that are important to this story — there are the ones that lead or warn, like a prediction, and there are signs that allow us to interpret the past.

Sometimes those signs are so upsetting, they lead us to an untimely death, and I'm not talking about Minnie here. My father died on a Monday. Just a little over a week after Minnie died. Her death was too much for him.

~Christ Edens~

Christ Edens proprietor of the Farmers Home Hotel at 215 First Avenue died Monday morning at 2 o'clock at the home of his son-in-law, William Seamer, of Elvira. Mr. Edens had gone to Elvira a week ago to attend the funeral services of his daughter, the late Mrs. Seamer, and was taken ill with pneumonia which developed into lung fever. He was 69 years of age, having celebrated his birthday anniversary three weeks ago.

Mr. Edens leaves to mourn his death his wife, and three sons, Will and John Edens of Elvira, and Christ Jr. at home, and seven daughters, Mrs. Gus Benson and Mrs. Otto Reyman of Elvira, Mrs. Joseph Wagner, Mrs. William Jensen, Mrs. Carl Ahrens, and Mrs. John Williams of this city and Miss Elsie Edens, residing at home. It is expected that the funeral services will be held Wednesday, and interment will be in the family lot at Springdale.

The old German woman told us to watch for signs. The kind that predict the future. The kind that can lead you down the wrong path. If there's one thing I learned from all of this, it's that the signs aren't always in my language. And sometimes the signs contradict each other; there are countless things talking. The world is a complex place. There might be an order out there somewhere, but it's so beyond our comprehension, that we may as well be ants trying to control the direction of automobile traffic. We interpret omens to give us the feeling that we have some control. The reality, though, is that this is just a feeling. There is no control, unless it's the power to let go of the illusion and just *experience*.

As far as interpreting the past goes... well... it's always possible to get a good picture as long as you are willing to check with multiple sources. Check every little thing — no matter how insignificant it seems. Like the flowers William said he threw in the ditch. After believing he was Minnie's killer for so many days, there was still a small amount of doubt in my mind. He was not completely innocent. Minnie's diary and his own confession made that clear. So I looked for those flowers the night that Papa died. Tears flowed down my cheeks and I needed to get away from more death, so I just went for a walk and found myself looking for them. There they were — saddened, soggy, and almost wilted beyond recognition. Signs are like that sometimes. But even when you find the signs, the best picture you will get is *good* — not great, not perfect, not complete.

The quest for the perfect picture of the past drives me now. Phinny and his booklet set me on the path. Minnie's death motivated me to stay on it. Now, I support myself by investigating other unsolved mysteries. I look at everybody and everything differently, looking for the hidden layers of the story. Even the innocent have something to hide.

And so that is what you have here. A good picture. I've tried my best. It's *here* as far as I can make it. But therein lies the problem. You are limited by the view I have given you. Now only one question remains... what do *you* think?

Acknowledgements

The thanks begin with Jan Hansen, Jone Trumpeter, and the many volunteers at the Clinton County Historical Museum. If it were not for your research, I wouldn't have seen those old newspaper clippings that got this all started.

Much thanks to Jeanne Rogis who shared her copy of *Murder and Mayhem in Clinton County, Iowa.*

To my students (past and present) whose enthusiasm for the story helped fuel the completion of this project.

To the reporters who wrote the articles in the first place. No offense intended… it just worked out that way. Rest in peace.

To my sister Sara, cousin T.J., and my friends Paul, Dave, Delphine, Theresa, Kevin, Chris, Jen, Linda, Vicki and others who showed curiosity, asked questions, offered suggestions, and listened.

Kris McGuire — Thank you for pushing me in new directions professionally and personally. Sometimes I didn't want to go, but I was always glad to get there.

To my uncle Dennis who used his obsession with ancestry to do a little digging for me.

Aunt Mary and Ken McMain — thanks for supporting the arts!

Shout out to Nancy who was brave enough to lead a class of eighth graders around a cemetery and her hometown. Thanks for the photos!

To the Hulls who were willing to open their door to me on a whim. Thanks for showing me the place and for sharing a few rumors that gave me some meaty ideas.

Thank you to Jean Rickertsen for being willing to dig through the trunks of your family history. The front cover photo is perfect!

To my extended family who fostered a love of old stories by sharing their own.

Kirstin, thanks for the German translation! Having that connection to the "old country" was important to me.

To Mom and Dad for listening, reading, suggesting, questioning, and encouraging me in countless ways. Thanks to Dad for tracking down that dollar! Thanks to Mom for the penmanship I could never match and for traipsing around the wrong graveyard with me in frigid temperatures.

Elaine — Infinite thanks for showing by example, the true meaning and value of patience.

To my boys — For being considerate when I was back in time. For asking, "Is it done yet?" That question helped prod me along. Thanks for adding your ideas and artwork. Watching you create is one of my biggest joys in life.

Christine Gilroy — Thank you for so many things. My editor, my friend, my coach. I'll never type another ellipsis without thinking of you. I could rave about you for another page, but "we've got a deadline to meet!"

And most of all to my husband, Eddie. I could write another page about everything you have done to help me. For the late nights, brainstorming, puzzle forming, voice, revising, editing, chauffeuring, handwriting, and drawing. Thanks for giving me the courage to walk up to that door. You are my greatest supporter and coach, and I love you.

Author's Note

At first, it was about the articles. A co-worker handed me a locally published *Murder and Mayhem in Clinton County, Iowa.* The book contained news articles from the early 1900s — all having to do with solved and unsolved murders in this small chock of Iowa. The Clinton County Historical Society sponsored the project spearheaded by Jan Hansen and Jone Trumpeter. These ladies perused old microfiche in pursuit of the mad mixture of foul play that took place in our once-rumored "Murder Capital of the World."

To tell the truth, I don't remember much about the other cases. One caught my attention and harnessed it for good — the death of a young woman named Wilhelmina Seamer.

Wilhelmina, known locally as Minnie, was no doubt the victim of foul play. Too many facts of the case made her suicide-by-hanging look highly unlikely.

Her husband's whereabouts around the time of her death (late Friday evening, June 20, 1913) remain sketchy. Local gossip claims the relationship was strained but none agreed on the reason. Their hired man disappeared soon after Minnie died. What did he know? Was he guilty? Was he even alive? A mile and a quarter away from the barn in which Minnie was hanged, another barn burned to the ground around the same time. This one, owned by her brother John Edens, was reportedly struck by lightning during the severe rainstorm that pummeled the area since that afternoon, turning all to mud — the same mud that should have been all over Minnie's stocking feet and floor length nightgown as she hanged — completely clean. No one actually heard lightning hit the barn, either. Was the fire merely a decoy?

Minnie and her brother John lived in a township made up of scattered family farms, a smith, grocer, creamery, saloon and hotel, and a smattering of other businesses and homes that made up the boardwalk of Elvira. All residents flocked to the barn fire at John's place to establish the only fire department there was — an impromptu bucket brigade. No one saw or heard what happened to Minnie Seamer that night.

At least no one innocent, that is.

Author Q and A

What was the genesis of this book?

It's difficult to determine the exact starting point. Initially, I became interested in those old newspaper articles as a way of engaging my students in history, critical thinking, and creative writing. After sifting out facts from rumors, I challenged the kids to create a theory that stuck to what we knew for sure. This resulted in a classroom filled with questions and brainstormed ideas posted everywhere. We were a veritable investigation crew. Trying to find an answer that covered all the bases, like William's whereabouts the night of her death and his strange movements in the days following, was like that old game Whac-a-Mole. Just when we thought we'd answered one question, two more cropped up. Students chose a theory they felt was the best. From there, they created some type of fictional "document" to support their theory — like a diary entry, a letter, a coroner's report, or a receipt. Over the years, I'd toyed with several of my own "documents." I suppose I became obsessed with finding the one theory that successfully answered all those questions. I needed to solve the puzzle. This morphed into a much more concerted effort to root out a full story.

How much of this is true?

When it comes down to it, what is truth? The process of doing this has made me think long and hard about that idea. At one point, people thought the world was flat. Sometimes "truth" gets in the way of possibility. There is always room for revision. The newspaper articles really are straight from two local publications. I forced myself to stick to the facts as presented there, and I had to do a lot more digging into the history of Clinton County, Iowa, to make the time period come alive. Like thousands of other German immigrants, Minnie's parents came to Iowa in the 1880s. My uncle actually found their names on the manifest at Ellis Island. The archives of the historical museum in Clinton and various books published on the history of this area helped me to infuse objects, travel, food, and culture with my theory. Little things like the boxing club, rag-rug socials, and the fair are all based on elements of truth. I imagined finding Minnie's diary entries in the attic of the old house; those, however, are entirely fictional.

The first chapter begins with a plane crash and the first mention of the importance of signs. Why did you begin this way?

The Clinton County Fair always takes place in my own hometown of DeWitt. When I was digging into the history of Clinton County, I came across the picture of Louis Rosenbaum and his plane at our fair 100 years ago. This tragedy was the first aviation fatality in the state of Iowa and took place only a few years before Minnie's death. I decided that it was likely Minnie and William actually did attend the fair and see the event first-hand. I knew I wanted the first chapter to begin with an element of superstition. After that, it all just came together.

Superstitions and compulsions play a big role in the book. To what extent are these based on culture and experience?

There is definitely a connection to culture there, and some personal experience influences it as well. I actually found old German "spells" that outlined things women could do to get pregnant. It drew me in to other superstitions – beliefs about numbers, death, and prayer. I decided this was one way to reflect the time period and the many German immigrants in this area of Iowa. As far as compulsions are concerned, I grew up harboring mildly annoying routines that caused me to do things for no apparent reason. I had to go out the same door I came in or bad luck would occur, I sorted all my stuffed animals into a certain arrangement before going to bed or my pets would die, and clothes had to be put away in a very particular manner or someone I loved would get hurt. Ridiculous thoughts like these come to mind occasionally, and I have to beat them off with a cudgel. I wanted to build a character that had debilitating obsessive-compulsive disorder before anyone even knew what it was.

How long did it take you to write?

I played around with ideas — documents and narration for several years before I made up my mind to see the whole thing through until the end. The last three years I've really worked on it wholeheartedly, mostly in the summertime when I'm not teaching.

What inspired the Table of Contents?

Before I even knew that Elsie was going to be the narrator, I decided that I wanted someone to be an investigator. I looked up "private investigator 1900" and found an old pamphlet for a private investigator's school that claimed, "World's Greatest School — Our Lessons Best — Easy to Learn." Thanks to a collector of investigative memorabilia, I had a starting point for the table of contents. I changed the order and some of the chapter headings, but it is mostly inspired by this antique pamphlet.

Was there really an Elsie Edens who became a private investigator?

Minnie did have a much younger sister named Elsie, but she died at an early age. For the most part, Elsie's character is totally fictional. She is an amalgamation of the brave and spunky girls that I teach who are not willing to quit when things get tough.

Is there anything to William's participation in the black market?

I owe this tidbit to the couple who live in William and Minnie's old house. They told me about the layout of the farm back then, the history of the house and its many renovations, the way Elvira sprawled into a "boardwalk" of stores and homes, and stories surrounding William. Due to the creation of The Pure Food and Drug Act of 1906, farmers were forced to do business much differently than in the past. These regulations caused a big uproar in our area. William Seamer took a lead role in protecting the interests of the local farmers and helped to establish a black market beef operation.

What was the hardest thing about writing this book?

That's an easy one. I had a very difficult time deciding on a narrator. I thought I wanted primary documents to tell the whole tale originally. In an early draft, Minnie was the main narrator through letters she wrote to her mother and Elsie, but I had trouble connecting with the conflict from this angle. There were certain things that just couldn't come through the way I wanted them to, so I scrapped that as an option. I also played around with another side to the story altogether and wrote a few chapters from the perspective of the "freak show" owner Stan Polanski in the Description chapter. Poor Polanski and his employees were pared down to a single paragraph. Then I wrote from the perspective of a hired private investigator. This character didn't have enough personal connection. Gradually Elsie surfaced as an option. The only thing that bothered me about her was the fact that the real Elsie died before any of this even happened. I was so adamant about sticking to the facts that I didn't seriously consider her for a long time. Then one night I decided to try writing a chapter from her perspective. I liked her voice so much that all other options fell off the table.

You mentioned that Elsie was inspired by some of your students, and bits of Minnie's personality came from your own experience. What about the other characters?

Walter is a little bit of each of my boys. An uncle of mine was the basis for William — at least the quiet part. Minnie's sisters Mary and Melinda are the composite of the few rumormongers that undermine a wholesome concept of community. Mama is a blend of my cantankerous Aunt Janet and my Great-grandma

Martha Kaszinski. Janet had a my-way-or-the-highway approach to life. Great-grandma Martha came to the United States from Germany when she was 16. She had a thick accent and head-strong ways. John is who I imagine my Great-uncle Eddie Kaszinski was at a young age. Eddie played the accordion, looked out for family and friends, and had a lighthearted personality. He always played jokes and kidded around, but as far as I know he never helped bury a dead body.

For more information on

Seeking Signs

and the
true events that inspired
this story please visit
www.staciangelinamercado.com

Made in the USA
Charleston, SC
15 June 2013